美國 日常生活口語

PRACTICAL ENGLISH FOR DAILY LIFE

Helping You Learn English The Easy Way

邊學邊用，地道美語讓您溝通無憂
國英，粵英逐句講解

Customer Hotline(客户熱綫): **888-862-1018**
Publisher: Times Publishing （NY） Ltd.
時代出版社（紐約）出版

目　録 Contents

英文字母 & 國際音標 Alphabets & IPA /1

數字 Numbers /2

日常生活 Daily Life

打招呼 Greeting /4

起床 Get Up /5

就寢 Go to Bed /7

家務 Housework /8

在家用餐 Eat in /10

日期與時間 Date & Time /12

天氣 Weather /14

問路 Asking for Directions /15

出行 Going Out /17

在銀行 At the Bank /20

在郵局 At the Post Office /22

在醫院 At the Hospital /23

美容 Beauty /30

美發 Hair Dressing /32

健康 Health /34

戀愛 Love（表白 Express Love、拒絕 Rejection、約會 Date、分手 Break Up） /36

婚姻 Marriage（結婚 Getting Married、離婚 Divorce） /45

聊天 Chat（社會 About Society、生活 About Life、雜七雜八 Odds and Ends） /53

拜訪 Visit /65

報警 Police Report（信用卡丟失 Loss of Credit Card、搶劫 Robbery、盜匪 Burglary、急救電話 Emergency Calls） /67

交通事故 Car Accident /70

工　作　Work

辦公室　At the Office /73
客户　About Customers /77

電　話　Phone Calls

打電話　Make Telephone Calls /82
接電話　Answer the Phone /83
電話留言　Leaving a Message /84
打錯電話　Dialing a Wrong Number /85

娛　樂　Entertainments

購物　Shopping（超市 Supermarket、便利店 Convenience Store、商場 Department Store） /87
運　動　Exercise /98
健身房　Gym /100
看電影　Seeing a Movie /102
唱 K　KTV /105
音樂會　Concert /106
酒吧　Bar /110
公園　Park /114

旅　行　Travel

搭乘交通工具　Transportation Tool /119
訂票　Booking a Ticket /120
簽證　Visa /121
體檢 & 檢疫　Physical & Quarantine /122
入境　Immigration /123
遺失行李　Lost Baggage /125
海關申報　Customs Declaration /127
機場旅游資訊
Airport Travel Information /129
機位查詢、確認
Confirm the Reservation /132
機場用語　At the Airport /134
住宿　Staying in A Hotel /136
用餐　In a Restaurant /141
觀光　Sightseeing /148

情　緒　Moods

高興　Happy /151
驚訝　Surprise /155
感動　Moved /156
自信　Confident /157
無聊　Boring /158
生氣　Angry /159
爲難　Embarrassed /161
害羞　Shy /162
難過　Sad /163

交　談　Conversation

同意　Agree /165
反對　Object /168
拒絕　Reject /171
請求　Request /175
商量　Discuss /178
責備　Blame /181
道歉　Apologize /184
道謝　Thank /187
抱怨　Complain /190

附　録　Appendix

美國節假日
US Holidays and Festivals /193
諺語　Proverbs /194
警告 / 提示　Warnings / Notices /204

本書編排與使用

1 點擊本書封面上的有聲標志，開啓本書有聲內容。

點擊內文頁右上角的語言鍵，選擇您需要的語言。

（注：如不選擇，您將無法聽取正文語音。）

2 點擊使用說明頁上的音量調節鍵，可以調節音量大小；

點擊MP3播放鍵上的各個按鈕，開啓相對應按鈕的功能。

3 本書共分爲七大主題，涉及生活、工作、娛樂等方面，內容全面具體，句子精煉實用。本書會是你在美國衣食住行、交友游玩的好幫手，它不僅僅可供你平日學習、查閱，還可以在你出行時隨身攜帶，隨時查找你想要表達的句子，并且有好學寶點讀筆幫你解決發音問題，點到哪裏讀哪裏，即學即用。

注：粵語部分語音不與文字對照，衹按口語習慣録音。

每個小主題都設計有不同顏色的索引，方便讀者查閱。

英、中、粵三個語言鍵，點擊任一個全書內容即發相應的語言的語音，學習者可以快速融入相應的語言環境，且不同語言間的切換方便快捷。

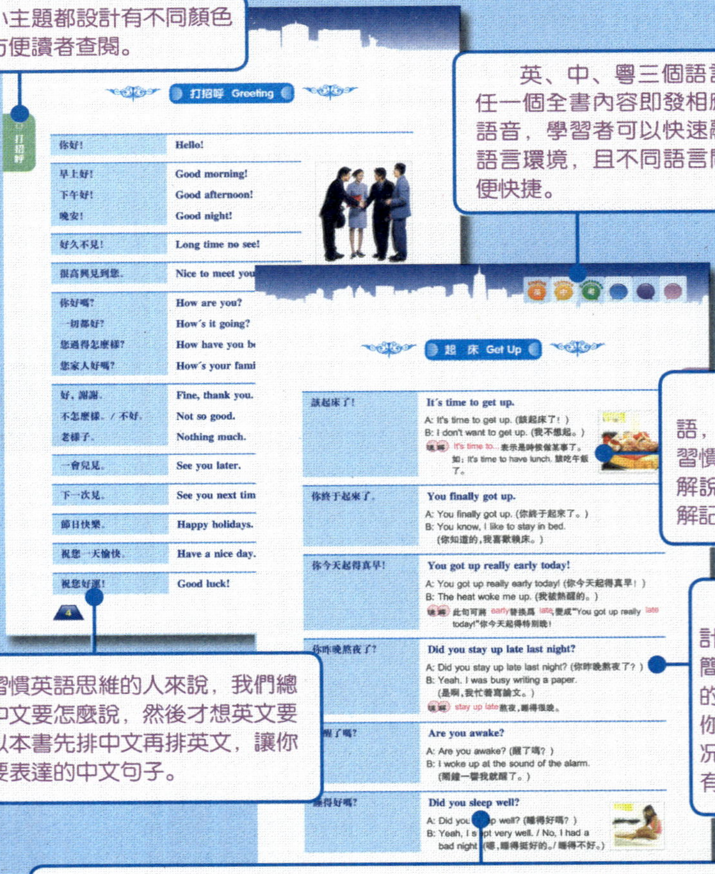

對相關的短語，固定搭配，習慣用語等進行解說，幫助你理解記憶。

根據句子設計的情景對話，簡短實用。書中的情景可能就是你即將遇到的情況，好好記着，有備無患。

對于不習慣英語思維的人來說，我們總是首先想到中文要怎麼說，然後才想英文要怎麼說。所以本書先排中文再排英文，讓你方便查找想要表達的中文句子。

與中文對應的英文表達，編者精心挑選常用表達，讓你說一口地道的口語。一些句子有多種表達方式，編者也在旁邊增加了這些相同的表達，豐富你的句型，積累多樣性的句子。

英文字母 Alphabets

大寫	A B C D E F G H I J K L M N O P Q R S T U V W X Y Z
小寫	a b c d e f g h i j k l m n o p q r s t u v w x y z

國際音標 IPA

英語國際音標表

單元音	短元音	[i] [ə] [ɔ] [u] [ʌ] [e] [æ]
	長元音	[i:] [ə:] [ɔ:] [u:] [ɑ:]
雙元音		[ei] [ai] [ɔi] [au] [əu] [iə] [ɛə] [uə]
清濁成對的輔音	清輔音	[p] [t] [k] [f] [θ] [s] [ts] [tr] [ʃ] [tʃ]
	濁輔音	[b] [d] [g] [v] [ð] [z] [dz] [dr] [ʒ] [dʒ]
其它輔音		[h] [m] [n] [ŋ] [l] [r] [j] [w]

數字

數　字 Numbers

One	一	Twenty	二十
Two	二	Twenty-one	二十一
Three	三	Twenty-two	二十二
Four	四	Twenty-three	二十三
Five	五	Thirty	三十
Six	六	Thirty-one	三十一
Seven	七	Forty	四十
Eight	八	Fifty	五十
Nine	九	Sixty	六十
Ten	十	Seventy	七十
Eleven	十一	Eighty	八十
Twelve	十二	Ninety	九十
Thirteen	十三	Hundred	一百
Fourteen	十四	One Hundred and Sixty	一百六十
Fifteen	十五	One Thousand	一千
Sixteen	十六	Eighteen-Hundred	一千八百
Seventeen	十七	Ten Thousand	一萬
Eighteen	十八	One Hundred Thousand	十萬
Nineteen	十九	Million	百萬

Daily Life
【日常生活】

- 打招呼
- 起　床
- 就　寢
- 家　務
- 在家用餐
- 日期與時間
- 天　氣
- 問　路
- 出　行
- 在銀行
- 在郵局
- 在醫院
- 美　容
- 美　發
- 健　康
- 戀　愛
  - 表　白
  - 拒　絕
  - 約　會
  - 分　手
- 婚　姻
  - 結　婚
  - 離　婚
- 聊　天
  - 社　會
  - 生　活
  - 雜七雜八
- 拜　訪
- 報　警
  - 信用卡丟失
  - 搶　劫
  - 盜　匪
  - 急救電話
- 交通事故

打招呼 Greeting

你好!	Hello!
早上好! 下午好! 晚安!	Good morning! Good afternoon! Good night!
好久不見!	Long time no see!
很高興見到您。	Nice to meet you.
你好嗎? 一切都好? 您過得怎麼樣? 您家人好嗎?	How are you? How´s it going? 回 How´s everything? How have you been? How´s your family?
好，謝謝。 不怎麼樣。/ 不好。 老樣子。	Fine, thank you. Not so good. Nothing much. 回 Nothing special.
一會兒見。	See you later.
下一次見。	See you next time.
節日快樂。	Happy holidays.
祝您一天愉快。	Have a nice day. 回 Have a good time.
祝您好運!	Good luck!

起 床 Get Up

該起床了!	**It´s time to get up.** A: It's time to get up. (該起床了!) B: I don't want to get up. (我不想起。) 注解 It's time to... 表示是時候做某事了。如: It's time to have lunch. 該吃午飯了。
你終于起來了。	**You finally got up.** A: You finally got up. (你終于起來了。) B: You know, I like to stay in bed. (你知道的,我喜歡賴床。)
你今天起得真早!	**You got up really early today!** A: You got up really early today! (你今天起得真早!) B: The heat woke me up. (我被熱醒的。) 注解 此句可將 early 替換爲 late,變成"You got up really late today!"你今天起得特別晚!
你昨晚熬夜了?	**Did you stay up late last night?** A: Did you stay up late last night? (你昨晚熬夜了?) B: Yeah. I was busy writing a paper. (是啊,我忙着寫論文。) 注解 stay up late 熬夜,睡得很晚。
你醒了嗎?	**Are you awake?** A: Are you awake? (醒了嗎?) B: I woke up at the sound of the alarm. (鬧鐘一響我就醒了。)
睡得好嗎?	**Did you sleep well?** A: Did you sleep well? (睡得好嗎?) B: Yeah, I slept very well. / No, I had a bad night. (嗯,睡得挺好的。/ 睡得不好。)

假日我睡到很晚。	**I get up late on holidays.**
你一向晚起嗎?	**Do you always get up late?** A: Do you always get up late? (你一向晚起嗎？) B: Yeah, because I'm a night person. (是的，因爲我是個夜猫子。) 注解 night person 也可以説 night owl。而 morning person 則是早起的人的意思。
我習慣睡到自然醒。	**I´m used to getting up naturally.** A: Does your family wake you up? (家人叫你起床嗎？) B: No, I'm used to getting up naturally. (不，我習慣睡到自然醒。) 注解 be used to doing something. 表示習慣做某事，常常做某事。
鬧鐘根本叫不醒我。	**The alarm clock can´t wake me up at all.** A: Didn't you hear the alarm clock go off? (你没聽到鬧鐘響嗎？) B: The alarm clock can't wake me up at all. (鬧鐘根本叫不醒我。) 注解 go off 是鬧鐘響的意思。
你用鬧鐘嗎?	**Do you use the alarm clock?**  A: Do you use the alarm clock? (你用鬧鐘嗎？) B: I use a cell phone as my alarm clock. (我用手機當鬧鐘。)
我做了個噩夢。	**I had a nightmare.** A: I had a nightmare. (我做了個噩夢。) B: It's all right now. (現在没事了。)
你還要睡多久?	**How long do you still need to sleep?** A: How long do you still need to sleep? (你還要睡多久？) B: I can sleep for a whole day if nothing happens. (没事的話我可以睡一整天。) 注解 sleep 睡覺。

就　寢 Go to Bed

晚安,好夢。	**Good night and sweet dreams.** A: Good night and sweet dreams. (晚安,好夢。) B: Good night. (晚安。)
明天八點叫醒我。	**Wake me up at eight tomorrow.** A: Wake me up at eight tomorrow. (明天八點叫醒我。) B: OK. (好的。)
你調鬧鐘了嗎?	**Do you set the alarm clock?** A: Do you set the alarm clock? (你調鬧鐘了嗎?) B: Yeah, I set it for 7:30. (調了七點半的。)
你通常幾點睡覺?	**What time do you usually go to bed?** A: What time do you usually go to bed? (你通常幾點睡覺?) B: I go to bed at ten p.m. every night. (我每晚十點睡覺。) 注解 go to bed 可以用 go to sleep 替換,兩者都是就寢的意思。 
刷牙了嗎?	**Have you brushed your teeth?** A: Have you brushed your teeth? (刷牙了嗎?) B: No, just a minute. (還沒,等一下。)
我睡前會喝杯牛奶。	**I drink a glass of milk before going to bed.** A: I drink a glass of milk before going to bed. (我睡前會喝杯牛奶。) B: That's good for sleep. (那有助于睡眠。)
我睡覺踢被子。	**I kick the quilt off while sleeping.** A: You've got a cold? (感冒了?) B: Yeah, I kick the quilt off while sleeping. (嗯,我睡覺踢被子。)

家　務 Housework

別忘了扔垃圾。

Don´t forget to take out the garbage.

A: Don't forget to take out the garbage.
(別忘了扔垃圾。)
B: I won't. (知道了)

注解 除了 garbage, rubbish 也表示垃圾。

把盤子擦幹。

Dry the dishes.

A: Dry the dishes. (把盤子擦幹。)
B: I will. (好的。)

你能幫我擺好餐具嗎?

Would you help me set the table?

A: Would you help me set the table?
(你能幫我擺好餐具嗎?)
B: I'm afraid not. I'm waiting for an important phone call.
(恐怕不行,我正在等一個很重要的電話。)

注解 set the table 是擺好餐具,而 clear the table 是收拾餐桌。

這是洗碗刷。

Here is a dish mop.

水開了!

The water is boiling!

A: The water is boiling! (水開了!)
B: OK. (知道了。)

幫我給植物澆水吧。

Help me water the plants.

A: Help me water the plants. (幫我給植物澆水吧。)
B: Can I water them when the game is over?
(等我玩完游戲行嗎?)

我正想打掃房子。

I´m going to clean up the house.

A: It's so dusty. (全是灰。)
B: I'm going to clean up the house.
(我正想打掃房子。)

我得拖地。	**I have to mop the floor.** A: Judy, would you like to watch a football game with us? (朱迪，你跟我們一起去看球賽嗎？) B: Yes, I'd love to, but I have to mop the floor. (我很想去，可是我得拖地。)
掃掃地。	**Please sweep the floor.** A: What do you want me to do? (我能幫你做什麼？) B: Please sweep the floor. (掃掃地。)
你能幫忙叠衣服嗎?	**Will you help me fold the clothes?** A: Will you help me fold the clothes? (你能幫忙疊衣服嗎？) B: Why don't you do it yourself? (你自己怎麽不叠？)
你能幫我熨那件襯衫嗎?	**Could you help me iron the shirt?** A: Could you help me iron the shirt? (你能幫我熨那件襯衫嗎？) B: I don't know how to use an iron. (我不會用熨鬥。) 注解 Iron 作名詞的時候是熨鬥的意思，作動詞時表示熨平。
去晾衣服。	**Please hang up the clothes to dry.** A: Please hang up the clothes to dry. (去晾衣服。) B: But I'm watching a film now. (可我正在看電影。)
你負責洗衣服。	**Your work is washing clothes.** A: What should I do? (我要做什麼？) B: Your work is washing clothes. (你負責洗衣服。)
你喂狗了嗎?	**Have you fed the dog?** A: Have you fed the dog? (你喂狗了嗎？) B: Yes. I'm taking it for a walk now. (喂了，現在我要帶它出去遛遛。)
擦一擦桌子。	**Please wipe the table.** A: Please wipe the table. (擦一擦桌子。) B: With a dry cloth or a damp one? (用幹布還是濕布？)

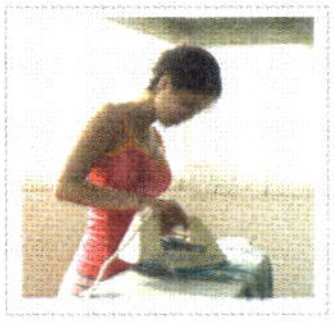

在家用餐 Eat in

晚餐吃什麼?	**What do we have for dinner?** A: What do we have for dinner? (晚餐吃什麼？) B: Seafood. (吃海鮮。) 注解 dinner 可以替換爲 breakfast, lunch 分別表示早餐，午餐。
把你的飯吃光。	**Finish up your food.** A: Finish up your food. (把你的飯吃光。) B: I am trying to. (我在努力中啦。) 注解 finish up：吃光。 
這個菜很好吃。	**It´s very tasty.** A: What do you think of this dish? (你覺得這個菜怎樣？) B: It's very tasty. (這個菜很好吃。) 注解 tasty 可以替換爲 delicious, yummy 均爲美味，好吃的意思。還可以替換 salty 咸的，fresh 新鮮的。
别灑出來了!	**Don´t spill it!** A: Don't spill it! (别灑出來了！) B: I'll be careful. (我會小心的。)
不許挑食。	**Don´t be picky.** A: I don't like carrots. (我不喜歡吃紅蘿卜。) B: Don't be picky. (不許挑食。)
還要多久可以吃飯?	**How soon will it be done?** A: How soon will it be done? (還要多久可以吃飯？) B: In ten minutes. (10 分鐘後。)
慢慢吃。	**Eat slowly.** A: Eat slowly. (慢慢吃。) B: I'm starving. (我好餓。)

現在可以吃晚飯了嗎?	**Can we have supper now?** A: Can we have supper now? (現在可以吃晚飯了嗎？) B: Wait a minute. Your sister is coming back soon. (等一下，姐姐馬上就回來了。)
你應該多吃一點。	**You should eat more.** A: You should eat more. (你應該多吃一點。) B: I can't swallow anything when I'm down. (心情不好我就吃不下。) 
我偶爾吃泡面當晚餐。	**Sometimes I have instant noodles for dinner.** A: Do you have instant noodles often? (你常吃泡面嗎？) B: Sometimes I have instant noodles for dinner. (我偶爾吃泡面當晚餐。)
你真的不吃晚餐嗎?	**Do you really not want any dinner?** A: Do you really not want any dinner? (你真的不吃晚餐嗎？) B: Yes. I'm so sleepy that I want to have a rest now. (不吃，我好困，要去睡覺了。)
開飯了。	**Come to eat.** A: Come to eat. (開飯了。) B: I'm coming. (來了。)
來不及吃早餐了。	**There´ll be no time for breakfast.**
請把胡椒給我。	**Pass me the pepper, please.** A: Pass me the pepper, please. (請把胡椒給我。) B: Here you are. (給你。)
不要爲我推遲開飯。	**Do not wait for me to have dinner.**
我不想吃午餐。	**I don´t feel like eating my lunch.**
不要一邊吃飯一邊看電視。	**No TV during dinner.**

日期與時間 Date & Time

今天幾號?	**What date is it today?** A: What date is it today? (今天幾號?) B: It's the ninth. (9 號。)
今天星期幾?	**What day is it?** A: What day is it? (今天星期幾?) B: It's Thursday. (星期四。)
8 月 23 日	**It´s August twenty–third.** A: When is your birthday? (你生日什麼時候?) B: It's August twenty-third. (8 月 23 日。) 
日期未定。	**The date is undecided.**
夏季有哪幾個月?	**What are the summer months?**
現在是幾月?	**What month is it?** A: What month is it? (現在是幾月?) B: It is April. (現在是四月。)
您要搭幾日幾點的飛機?	**What time and date would you like to make this flight?**
請核實一下日期。	**Please check the date.**
我等了幾分鐘。	**I waited for a few minutes.**
現在幾點?	**What time is it now?** A: What time is it now? (現在幾點?) B: It's three o'clock. (三點。)

2 點 15 分。	**It´s a quarter past two.** A: Could you tell me the time? (可以告訴我現在幾點嗎？) B: It's a quarter past two. (2 點 15 分。) 注解 還可以說"It's two fifteen."
6 點半。	**It´s half past six.** 注解 相當于"It's six thirty."
那表快 5 分鐘。	**The clock is five minutes fast.** A: The clock is five minutes fast. (那表快 5 分鐘。) B: Thank you for telling me. (謝謝你告訴我。) 注解 把 fast 替換爲 slow 可以表示那表慢 5 分鐘。

常見詞 Common Words

Year	年	Monday	星期一
Month	月	Tuesday	星期二
Day	日、天	Wednesday	星期三
Last year	去年	Thursday	星期四
Next month	下個月	Friday	星期五
Morning	早晨	Saturday	星期六
Noon	中午	Sunday	星期日
Afternoon	下午	January	一月
Evening	傍晚	February	二月
Night	晚上	March	三月
Late night	深夜	April	四月
Mid-night	凌晨	May	五月
Today	今天	June	六月
Tomorrow	明天	July	七月
The day after tomorrow	後天	August	八月
The day before yesterday	前天	September	九月
Yesterday	昨天	October	十月
Week	星期、周	November	十一月
Weekend	周末	December	十二月

天 氣 Weather

今天天氣怎樣?	How´s the weather today?
紐約冬天天氣怎樣?	What´s the weather like in New York in winter?
天氣老是這樣嗎?	Is the weather always like this?
我希望天氣總是這麼好。	I hope the weather stays this way.
今天的氣溫是多少?	What´s the temperature today?
明天將是個晴天。	It´s going to be fine tomorrow.
今天很熱,是嗎?	Very hot today, isn´t it?
要下雨了。	It´s going to rain.
我看這雨不會下很久的。	I don´t think the rain would last long.
雨下得真大。	It´s raining heavily.
今天會下雪。	It´s going to snow today.
今天比昨天冷多了。	It´s much colder than yesterday.
今天氣溫接近 100 華氏度。	It´s almost 100 degrees today.
明天氣溫將會降到零下。	The temperature will drop below zero tomorrow.

問路 Asking for Directions

打擾一下，請問博物館怎麼走?

Excuse me, could you tell me how to get to the museum?

A: Excuse me, could you tell me how to get to the museum? (打擾一下，請問博物館怎麼走？)

B: Cross the street, then walk straight ahead, and you'll see it. (過馬路後往前走就看到了。)

注解 museum 可以替換其它的地方，如 supermarket (超市), park (公園), zoo (動物園), library (圖書館)等。

我想去星巴克咖啡館。請問怎麼去?

I´d like to go to Starbucks. How can I get there?

A: I'd like to go to Starbucks. How can I get there? (我想去星巴克咖啡館。請問怎麼去？)

B: Do you know where the Golden Age Bookstore is? (你知道黃金書店在哪裏嗎？)

請問這是哪裏?

Can you tell me where the place is?

請問我在地圖上的什麼地方?

Please tell me where I am on this map.

A: Please tell me where I am on this map. (請問我在地圖上的什麼地方？)

B: On the map, you're right here. (你在地圖上的這裏。)

我必須過馬路嗎?

Do I need to cross the road?

你走錯方向了。

You´re going in the wrong direction.

我該往哪個方向走?

In which direction should I go?

A: In which direction should I go? (我該往哪個方向走？)

B: To the west. (往西走。)

左轉還是右轉?

Turn left, or turn right?

我想我迷路了。	**I´m afraid I´ve gotten lost.** A: I'm afraid I've gotten lost. (我想我迷路了。) B: Don't worry. I'll show you the way. (別擔心，我給你指路。)
這附近有畫廊嗎?	**Is there a gallery near here?** A: Is there a gallery near here? (這附近有畫廊嗎?) B: Once you pass the traffic light, you'll be there. (過了這個紅綠燈就到了。)
郵局在哪裏?	**Where´s the post office?** A: Where's the post office? (郵局在哪裏?) B: Go straight for two blocks. (一直走到第二個街區。)
我第一次來這兒。	**I´m new here.** A: Excuse me, is there a cafe near by? (請問一下，這附近是不是有家咖啡店?) B: Sorry, I'm new here. (不好意思，我第一次來這兒。)
那裏遠嗎?	**Is it far?** A: Is it far? (那裏遠嗎?) B: Not far, only a five minute walk. (不遠，走路五分鐘就到了。) 
這是條近路嗎?	**Is it the shortcut?**
要多久?	**How long will it take?** A: How long will it take? (要多久?) B: It will take about half an hour by walking. (走路要大概半個小時。)
走路到得了嗎?	**Can I walk there?** A: Can I walk there? (走路到得了嗎?) B: You'd better take a taxi. (最好坐計程車去。)
我在哪兒?	**Where am I?**
我在哪條街?	**What street am I on?**

出 行 Going Out

坐 4 號車能到市政廳嗎?

Can I take No.4 bus to City Hall?

A: Can I take No.4 bus to City Hall?
(坐 4 號車能到市政廳嗎?)

B: Yes, go straight when you get off the bus.
(可以,下車後直走就到了。)

坐地鐵要多久?

How long will it take by subway?

A: How long will it take by subway? (坐地鐵要多久?)

B: About twenty minutes. (二十分鐘左右。)

注解 by subway 可以替換爲 by bus (公車), by car (汽車), by train(地鐵)等等。

早班車是幾點?

When is the morning shift?

A: When is the morning shift? (早班車是幾點?)

B: Six o'clock everyday. (每天 6 點。)

注解 morning shift 可以替換成 night shift,表示末班車。

多長時間一趟車?

How often does the bus come?

A: How often does the bus come?
(多長時間一趟車。)

B: The bus comes every twenty minutes. (20 分鐘一趟。)

我該在哪站下車?

Where should I get off?

A: Where should I get off? (我該在哪站下車?)

B: You can get off at this station. (你可以在這一站下車。)

注解 下車是 get off,上車是 get on。

這輛車到火車站嗎?

Is this bus heading for the subway station?

A: Is this bus heading for the subway station?
(這輛車到地鐵站嗎?)

B: Not directly. You need to change buses.
(不能直接到,要換乘。)

售票處在哪兒?

Where´s the ticket counter?

A: Where's the ticket counter? (售票處在哪兒？)
B: Go ahead, then turn left. (直走左轉。)

車票多少錢?

How much is the fare?

A: How much is the fare? (車票多少錢？)
B: What kind of tickets do you want? (你要哪種車票?)

下一站是哪兒?

What´s the next stop?

我要在哪兒換乘?

Where should I change?

A: Where should I change? (我要在哪兒換乘？)
B: You should transfer to Bus M1 at the next station.
(在下一站換成 M1 路車。)

請問還有幾站?

How many stops are left?

哪裏可以坐計程車?

Where can I get a taxi?

A: Where can I get a taxi? (哪裏可以坐計程車？)
B: You can take a taxi at the next corner.
(你可以在下個拐角處坐。)

注解 cab 也表示計程車，在口語中經常使用。

我打電話叫計程車了。

I already called a taxi.

A: Be quick. I already called a taxi.
(快點！我打電話叫計程車了。)
B: Coming right up. (馬上來。)

我要去機場。

I´m going to the airport.

A: Where are you heading? (你去哪兒？)
B: I'm going to the airport. (我要去機場。)

我要到上面這個地址。

I want to get to this address.

A: Where would you like to go? (你要去哪裏？)
B: I want to get to this address. (我要到上面這個地址。)

請開快一點，我在趕時間。

I´m in a hurry, please drive a little faster.

是不是走錯路了?	**Did we go the wrong way?** A: Did we go the wrong way? (是不是走錯路了?) B: No. There will be less traffic by going this way. (沒有。走這條路比較不塞車。)
這樣子好像繞了遠路。	**It seems like this is the long way to go.** A: It seems like this is the long way to go. (這樣子好像繞了遠路。) B: Is there a shortcut? (有近路嗎?)
請走不會塞車的路。	**Please take a road that will avoid the traffic.** A: Please take a road that will avoid the traffic. (請走不會塞車的路。) B: It is rush hour, there is traffic everywhere. (上下班高峰期,哪裏都塞車。)
請在拐角處停車。	**Please stop at the corner.**
請在這裏停下。	**Please drop me off here.**
我要付多少錢?	**How much should I pay?**
請給我收據。	**Please give me a receipt.** A: Do you need a receipt? (需要收據嗎?) B: Please give me a receipt. Thank you. (請給我收據。謝謝。)
要麻煩你找錢。	**Sorry, but I need change.**
我想租輛車。	**I want to rent a car.** A: I want to rent a car. (我想租輛車。) B: What type do you want? (你想要什麼車型?)
租金是多少?	**What´s the rental fee?**
如果我的租車期限過了,這將要加多少錢呢?	**How much does it cost if I go over the rental period?**

在銀行 At the Bank

辦理信用卡的手續是什麼?	What is the procedure to apply for a credit card?
您每天可以用信用卡支取現金兩次。	You can withdraw cash with the credit card twice a day.
我要把一些錢存入我的賬户。	I´d like to deposit some money to my account.
你們這裏辦理存款嗎?	Do you deal with deposits here?
請寫下您的名字,你的賬號,及您想存款數額。	Please write down your name, your account number and the amount you want to put in on this deposit number.
那麼,我得在賬户中存多長時間才可以取款呢?	How long do I have to keep the money in the account?
對不起,讓我重點一下。	Sorry. Let me count them again.
你介意告訴我怎麼從我的賬户取款嗎?	Would you mind telling me how to withdraw money from my account?
沿墻的那張桌上有些取款單。	There are some withdrawal slips on the table along the wall.
請您去填寫一份,説明你要取多少,日期。	Please go and fill one out, stating the amount you want to withdraw, date.
在簽名欄下簽名。	Sign under the signature line.
您帶存折了嗎?	Have you got your passbook with you?

小姐，您要多少面值的鈔票?	How do you want it, miss?
請給我 1,000 元面額爲一百元的鈔票，其餘的給我零錢。	Please let me have $1,000 in hundreds and the rest in small change.
我想匯些錢到中國。	I need to send some money to China.
我們將從你賬户中扣除這項費用。	We´ll charge this item to your account.
我們可以發付款單到銀行。	We could send a payment order to that bank.
這是匯款申請書。	Here is the application form for remittance.
您要匯多少?	How much would you like to remit?
我想開立一個銀行賬户。	I´d like to open a bank account.
你想開哪種帳號?	What kind of accounts did you have in mind?
我們不收任何手續費。	There isn´t any service charge.
請您和我説説這方面的事好嗎?	Can you give me some information?
有没有存款最小餘額的限制?	Is there a minimum balance requirement?
這裏的'密碼'是什麼意思?	What does it mean by pin number?
我們可以用它來辨認您的身份。	We use it to verify your identity.

在郵局 At the Post Office

這個快郵包裹的額外郵資是多少?	What´s the surcharge on this express parcel?
我想把這包裹寄往加拿大。	I want to mail this parcel to Canada.
打擾一下,我要寄封信,你能告訴我郵編嗎?	Excuse me. I´d like to send this letter. Could you tell me the zip code?
你要往哪兒寄?	Where are you sending to?
我想給這包東西保險五十美元。	I´d like to insure this package for 50 dollars.
請用快郵寄送這個包裹。	Please send this parcel off special delivery.
請郵送這祇大衣箱,貨到付款。	Please send this trunk cash on delivery.
請您先簽收。	Please endorse it first.
請在這張匯票上簽名。	Please sign this order.
請問可不可以把這張匯款單兌現?	Can I have this money order cashed, please?
昨天我拿到一張郵包到達通知單。我能在這兒領取嗎?	I got a parcel arrival notice yesterday. Can I get it here?
我們不接受體積太大的包裹。	We don´t accept bulky packages.

在醫院 At the Hospital

要叫醫生嗎?	**Do you need a doctor?** A: Do you need a doctor? (要叫醫生嗎?) B: No, thanks. I'll be all right soon. (不,謝謝。我很快就沒事的。)
要叫救護車嗎?	**Should I call an ambulance?**
挂號處在哪裏?	**Where´s the Registration?** A: Where's the Registration? (挂號處在哪裏?) B: It's near the main entrance. (在正門附近。)
請問我要看哪個科?	**Could you tell me which department I should register?** A: Could you tell me which department I should register? (請問我要看哪個科?) B: You should see the physician. (你應該看内科。)
我没有保險。	**I have no insurance.** A: Please show me your Insurance card. (可以出示您的保險卡嗎?) B: I have no insurance. (我没有保險。) 
我身體不舒服。	**I´m not feeling well.**
我覺得惡心,想吐。	**I feel nausea and vomiting.**
我難受。	**I feel sick.** A: What's wrong with you? (你怎麼了?) B: I feel sick. (我難受。)
我想預約斯通醫生。	**I´d like to make an appointment to see Dr. Stone.**

我明天能預約史密斯醫生看病嗎?	**May I see Dr. Smith tomorrow?** A: May I see Dr.Smith tomorrow? (我明天能預約史密斯醫生看病嗎?) B: Sorry. Dr.Smith is fully booked tomorrow. (抱歉,明天史密斯醫生的預約已經滿了。)
我胃痛。	**I feel a dull pain in the stomach.** A: You look pale. (你的臉色不好。) B: I feel a dull pain in the stomach. (我胃痛。) 注解 dull pain 是指隱隱作痛。 
我嗓子痛。	**I have a sore throat.**
我頭暈。	**I feel dizzy.**
我鼻塞。	**My nose is stuffed up.**
我流鼻涕,打噴嚏。	**I have a runny nose and sneezing.** A: I have a runny nose and sneezing. (我流鼻涕,打噴嚏。) B: Have a good rest! (好好休息吧!)
我咳嗽了一整晚。	**I coughed the whole night.** A: I coughed the whole night. (我咳嗽了一整晚。) B: You should go to see a doctor. (你應該去看醫生。)
我好像發燒了。	**I think I have a fever.** A: I think I have a fever. (我好像發燒了。) B: Let me take your temperature. (量一下體溫吧。)
我覺得不舒服。	**I´m not feeling well.**
我覺得很不舒服。	**I´m feeling very bad.**
我應該吃什麼樣的飲食?我需要吃特別的飲食嗎?	**What kind of food should I eat? Should I have a special diet?**

我最近感到不舒服。	I don´t feel well lately.
我該怎麼辦?	What should I do?
我需要住院嗎?	Should I stay in the hospital?
我的疼痛有些減輕。	The pain seems less.
它能很快痊愈嗎?	Will it go away soon?
我什麼時候再來?	When shall I come back?
這病會復發嗎?	Will there be a recurrence?
這藥有副作用嗎?	Does this medicine have any side–effects?
需要做手術嗎?	Will surgery be necessary?
很久才能恢復嗎?	Will it take long to recover?
可以在地上走走，鍛煉鍛煉嗎?	Is it all right to move around and do some exercises?
情況嚴重嗎?	Is it serious?
有危險嗎?	Is there any danger?
可能是什麼原因呢?	What could be the cause?
我若是再犯，該怎麼辦呢?	What should I do if I have another attack?
可能是什麼病呢?	What could it be?
你認爲怎樣?	What do you think?
沒有什麼好藥嗎?	Isn´t there any good medicine for it?

這是一種什麼藥呢？	What kind of medicine is this?
我不喜歡打針，能吃些口服藥嗎？	I hate injections. Can I take the medicine orally?
能治好麼？	Can it be cured?
能變壞嗎？	Will it get worse?
對于這種疼痛，有沒有辦法呢？	Can anything be done for the pain?
聽從你的意見。	Whatever you say.
這病傳染嗎？	Is it contagious?
我感到發困。	I feel sleepy.
我有痔瘡。	I have piles.
你有什麼事？	What can I do for you? What´s wrong with you?
我能幫你什麼忙嗎？	May I help you?
請坐下。	Please take a seat! Please sit down!
請等一等。	Wait a moment, please. Just a minute, please.
對不起，讓你久等了。	Sorry to have kept you waiting.
病情不嚴重。	It is not serious.
你需要卧床幾天。	You should stay in bed for a few days.
你很快就會好起來。	You´ll soon be all right.

不必顧慮。	Don´t worry. ▣ There is nothing to worry about.
你需要做一個全面檢查。	You need a thorough examination.
你需要在醫院裏住幾天。	You will have to stay in hospital for several days.
我們認爲你最好住進醫院來。	We think that you had better be hospitalized.
盡量放鬆保持鎮靜。	Try to relax and keep calm.
這一兩周內，你需要很注意。	You should be very careful for a week or two.

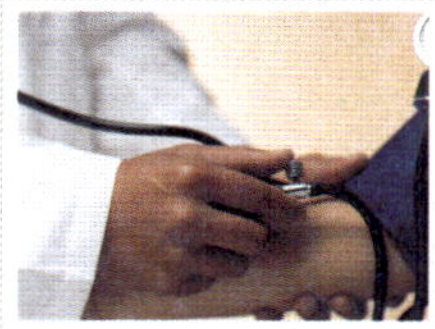

這藥對你肯定會很有效的。	I´m sure this medicine will help you a great deal.
恐怕痊愈將是一個很慢的過程。	Feeling well again is a rather slow process, I´m afraid.
你需要等 20 分鐘。	You will have to wait for twenty minutes.
徹底恢復需要一段很長時間。	Complete recovery will take a rather long time.
你需要定期來門診檢查。	You will have to come here for periodical check-ups.
我馬上就來。	I´ll come right away.
要是你覺得病加重了，就請馬上來門診。	If you feel worse, please come back to the clinic right away.
你要覺得難受，無論白天黑夜都趕緊上診所看去。	If you feel worried, don´t hesitate to go to the clinic anytime, day or night.

我去給你安排住院。	I´m going to make arrangements for your admission.
下次請帶翻譯來。	Please come with your interpreter next time.
你明白我的話嗎?	Do you understand what I´m saying?
你看在哪些方面還需要解釋呢?	Is there anything else you would like me to explain to you?
需要我再解釋一遍嗎?	Shall I explain it again?
要是情況還不見好,就請你再來門診吧。	If the trouble persists come back again.
不像有什麼嚴重情況,但還是要拍張 X 光肯定一下。	There doesn´t seem to be anything serious, but we´ll take an x-ray just to be certain.
請等一下,我們需要看一下 X 光(驗血)的結果。	Please wait until we get the result of the x-ray (blood test).
我建議你作理療。	I suggest that you get physiotherapy treatment.
你不舒服多久了?	How long have you been feeling unwell?
在您這樣歲數的人當中,這可太尋常了。	This is quite common among people of your age.
這種情況經常發生在你這樣歲數的人。	This often happens to people of your age.
這就經常出在你這種歲數上。	This often occurs at your age.
你吃的是什麼藥?	What medicine did you take?
你的胃有過燒心感嗎?	Do you suffer from heartburn stomachaches?

我建議你做些輕微的鍛煉。	I suggest you do some light exercises.
我建議你做一個療程的針灸。	I suggest you have a course of acupuncture.
明早查血以前不要吃東西。	Please don´t eat anything tomorrow morning before blood test.
你要補牙嗎?	Do you want to have your tooth filled?
請脫鞋,躺下。	Please take off your shoes and lie down.
請放鬆。	Please relax.
請深呼吸。	Please breathe deeply.
我給你量一下血壓。	Let me take your blood pressure.
你以前治過嗎?	Have you ever received any treatment before?
這種情況以前發生過嗎?	Has it happened before?
你覺得好些了嗎?	Are you feeling better?
疼痛減輕些了嗎?	Is the pain getting less?
你從什麼時候開始有這種痛的?	How long have you had this pain?
是什麼樣的痛?	What kind of pain is it?
請告訴我你過去的病史。	Please tell me something of your past illnesses.
你的尿裏有血嗎?	Is there any blood in your urine?

美 容 Beauty

我的皮膚容易過敏。

I have sensitive skin.

A: I have sensitive skin. (我的皮膚容易過敏。)

B: You should choose suitable care products. (你要選擇適合的護膚品。)

我一熬夜就長痘痘。

I break out in pimples if I stay up late.

A: How come you have so many pimples? (你怎麼長這麼多痘痘?)

B: I break out in pimples if I stay up late. (我一熬夜就長痘痘。)

我有黑眼圈。

I have dark circles under my eyes.

你變白了。

Your skin has become whiter.

A: Your skin has become whiter. (你變白了。)

B: I often apply a whitening facial mask. (我經常敷美白面膜。)

我的皮膚是幹性的。

I have dry skin.

A: I have dry skin. (我的皮膚是幹性的。)

B: You should work on moisturizing your skin. (你要加强皮膚的保濕。)

注解 oily 油性，normal 中性，sensitive 敏感性。

夏天出門我一定擦防曬霜。

I always put on sun block when I go out in summer.

我應該多久做一次深層清潔?

How often should I do deep cleaning?

A: How often should I do deep cleaning? (我應該多久做一次深層清潔?)

B: Once a month. (一個月一次。)

我想做面部美容。

I´d like a facial.

你怎麼保養皮膚?

How do you take care of your skin?

A: How do you take care of your skin?
(你怎麼保養皮膚？)

B: I think enough sleep is good for skin.
(我覺得睡眠充足皮膚就會好。)

我不經常化妝。

I don´t put on make–up often.

注解 light make-up 淡妝，heavy make-up 濃妝，nude make-up 裸妝。

這個面霜要怎麼用?

How can I apply this cream?

A: How can I apply this cream?
(這個面霜要怎麼用？)

B: You can use it after applying lotion.
(擦完乳液後用就可以了。)

我要美白保濕的化妝水。

I want a whitening and hydrating toner.

A: I want a whitening and hydrating toner. (我要美白保濕的化妝水。)

B: This one matches your skin. (這款適合你的皮膚。)

我想修眉。

I´d like to have my eyebrows trimmed.

我想做指甲。

I´d like to do my nails.

A: I'd like to do my nails. (我想做指甲。)

B: What color do you like? (你喜歡什麼顏色的？)

我要去角質。

I´d like to have my skin exfoliated.

我要化個晚宴妝。

I´d like to have an evening make–up for parties.

A: I'd like to have an evening make-up for parties.
(我想化個晚宴妝。)

B: Ok. This way, please. (好的。這邊請。)

我每天徹底卸妝。

I completely remove my make–up everyday.

A: I completely remove my make-up everyday.
(我每天徹底卸妝。)

B: That's a good habit. (這是個好習慣。)

美 發 Hair Dressing

我要洗頭。	**I want a shampoo.**
我要剪有劉海的。	**I´d like to cut my bangs.** A: How do you like your haircut? (你要怎麼剪？) B: I'd like to cut my bangs. (我要剪有劉海的。)
你打算留長頭發嗎?	**Are you going to wear your hair long?** A: Are you going to wear your hair long? (你打算留長頭發嗎？) B: Yeah. (是啊。)
長頭發容易打結。	**Long hair tangles easily.**
我的頭發很幹。	**My hair is very dry.** A: Do you use conditioner? (你用護發素嗎？) B: Yes. My hair is very dry. (用。我的頭發很幹。)
你覺得什麼發型適合我?	**What hairstyle do you feel will look good on me?** A: What hairstyle do you feel will look good on me? (你覺得什麼發型適合我？) B: How about this one? (這個怎樣？) 
這個長度可以嗎?	**Do you think it´s ok?** A: Do you think it's ok? (這個長度可以嗎？) B: Please cut it shorter. (請再剪短一點。)
我想剪頭發。	**I need a haircut.**
我要剪短發。	**I want to have my hair bobbed.** A: I want to have my hair bobbed. (我要剪短發。) B: How short? (多短？)

我想做個卷發。

I want to have my hair curled.

A: I want to have my hair curled. (我想做個卷發。)
B: What kind of curl do you like? (你想要哪種卷？)

我想染頭發。

I want my hair dyed.

A: I want my hair dyed. (我想染頭發。)
B: Ok. Please go this way to choose your favorite color first. (好的。請先到這邊選你喜歡的顏色。)

你覺得紅色怎樣?

What do you think of red?

A: What do you think of red? (你覺得紅色怎樣？)
B: Good. Red looks fashionable. (挺好的，紅色看起來很時尚。)

這個發型適合我嗎?

Do you think the hairstyle fits me?

A: Do you think the hairstyle fits me? (這個發型適合我嗎？)
B: You look more feminine in this hairstyle. (這個發型讓你更有女人味。)

我要拉直頭發。

I want my hair straightened.

A: I want my hair straightened. (我要拉直頭發。)
B: Would you like a trim? (要修一下嗎？)

我一個月換一次發型。

I change my hairstyle every month.

洗頭,做頭發要多少錢?

How much do you charge for a shampoo and set?

我想分在左邊。

I want it parted on the left.

A: Which way do you part your hair? (你頭發習慣分哪一邊？)
B: I want it parted on the left. (我想分在左邊。)

你可不可以把兩邊的頭發再剪掉一點?

Could you take a little bit more off the sides?

別把頭發剪得太短了。

Don´t cut the hair too short.

健康 Health

我一直都很健康。	**I have always been healthy.** A: I have always been healthy. (我一直都很健康。) B: How do you keep yourself in good health? (你是怎麽保持健康的？)
我從小就體弱多病。	**I have been weak and sickly since I was very young.** A: You're sick? (你又病了？) B: I have been weak and sickly since I was very young. (我從小就體弱多病。)
我經常感冒。	**I get a cold easily.** A: I get a cold easily. (我經常感冒。) B: You should do some exercise every day. (你應該每天做運動。)

我腸胃不好。	**I have indigestion.**
我怕打針。	**I´m afraid of needles.**
我討厭吃藥。	**I hate taking medicine.**
我吃完晚飯後就胃痛。	**I have stomachache after dinner.** A: What disease bothers you? (有什麽疾病困擾你嗎？) B: I have stomachache after dinner. (我吃完晚飯後就胃痛。)
我没有蛀牙。	**I don´t have cavities.**
你做過手術嗎?	**Have you ever had an operation?** A: Have you ever had an operation? (你做過手術嗎?) B: Never. (從來没有。)

生理期我會很不舒服。	**I feel very uncomfortable during my period.** A: Do you have menstrual pains? (你痛經嗎？) B: No, but I feel very uncomfortable during my period. (不會，但在生理期我會很不舒服。)
我覺得健康很重要。	**I think health is very important.**
我全身酸痛。	**My whole body aches.** A: My whole body aches. (我全身酸痛。) B: You may catch a cold. (你可能感冒了。)
我吃綜合維生素補充營養。	**I take multivitamines to supplement my diet.** A: I take multivitamines to supplement my diet. (我吃綜合維生素補充營養。) B: I think eating fresh vegetables and fruits is better for you. (我覺得你還是吃新鮮的蔬菜水果比較好。)
我每年做一次體檢。	**I have a physical examination every year.** A: Do you regularly have a physical examination? (你定期做身體檢查嗎？) B: I have a physical examination every year. (我每年做一次體檢。)
你覺得自己健康嗎?	**Do you think you´re healthy?** A: Do you think you're healthy? (你覺得自己健康嗎?) B: Yeah, everything is okay except headache. (除了頭痛，其它都很好。)
你擔心癌癥嗎?	**Do you worry about cancer?**
吸烟對健康有害。	**Smoking is not good for your health.**
我羨慕你的健康。	**I envy you your good health.**
少吃快餐。	**Eat less fast food.**
少吃肉多吃蔬菜。	**Eat less meat and more vegetables.**

戀 愛 Love

● 表 白 Express Love

我有話對你説。	**I want to talk to you.** A: I want to talk to you. (我有話對你説。) B: What's up? (怎麼啦?)
你現在有朋友嗎?	**Are you seeing anyone now?** A: Are you seeing anyone now? (你現在有朋友嗎?) B: Yeah, kind of. (嗯,怎麼説呢……) 注解 see 除了表示“看見”之外,還可表示“與……交往”。
你現在有男/女朋友嗎?	**Do you have a boyfriend / girlfriend now?**
我暗戀你有一段時間了。	**I have had a crush on you for some time now.** A: I have had a crush on you for some time now. (我暗戀你有一段時間了。) B: I never knew that before. (我從來没發現。) 注解 have a crush on...意爲:暗戀。
你使我神魂顛倒。	**I am crazy about you.** 注解 crazy about...,意爲:對……很着迷。
我愛你。	**I love you.**
我對你的愛是真心的。	**I love you from the bottom of my heart.**
我希望能得到你的愛。	**I hope to win your love.**
擁有你,就擁有了世界。	**Take you, take the world.**
我對你一見鍾情。	**I loved you at first sight.**

縱有千言萬語也無法表達我對你的愛。	**I love you more than I can say.**
我已經愛上你了。	**I am falling in love with you.** A: I am falling in love with you. (我已經愛上你了。) B: Really? I can hardly believe my ears! (真的嗎？我簡直不敢相信自己的耳朵。) 注解 fall in love with somebody. 意爲：愛上某人。
我會認真的保護你一輩子。	**I will protect you certainly attentively!**
擁有你，我是世界上最幸福的人!	**You make me the happiest man / woman in the world!**
在這個世界上，你是我的一切,擁抱你,我會擁有整個世界。	**In this small world, you are my all, embrace you and I will have the entire world.**
對于世界你也許衹是個人,但對于我,有了你,就相當于擁有了全世界!	**To the world you may be one person, but to me you may be the world.** 
你是我見到過的最美的女人。	**You´re the most beautiful woman I´ve ever seen.**
你是我喜歡的類型。	**You´re my type.** A: Why do you like me? (你爲什麼喜歡我?) B: You're my type. (你是我喜歡的類型。)
我深情的愛唯獨給你一個人。	**My passionate love is just for you.**
在我眼裏，你就是一位美麗的天使。	**You are like a beautiful angel in my eyes.**
愛情是盲目的。我愛你，不管貧窮或富有。	**Love is blind. I love you, poor or rich.**

每次見到你，你都更漂亮。	**You look prettier every time I see you.**
我全心全意愛你。	**I love you with all my heart.**
我愛你并不是因爲你是誰。	**I love you not for whom you are.**

我也喜歡你啊，就像你喜歡我一樣。	**For the same reason you like me, I like you, too.**
對你的愛,似海深。	**My love for you is as deep as the sea.**
我會永遠愛你的。	**I´ll love you forever!**
即使太陽從西邊出來，我對你的愛也不會改變。	**If the sun were to rise in the west, I´d never change my mind to love you forever.**
我想永遠和你在一起。	**I want to share my life with you.**
你是唯一一個能讓我開心快樂的人。	**You´re the only man / woman I could be happy with.**

● 拒 絕 Rejection

你不吸引我。	**You are not attractive to me.** A: I am crazy for you. (你使我神魂顛倒。) B: But you are not attractive to me. (但是你并不吸引我。)
我不喜歡你。	**I don´t like you.**
我們還可以做朋友。	**We still can be friends.** A: Can't we be lovers? (我們真的不能成爲戀人嗎？) B：No, we can't. But we still can be friends. (嗯,是的。但是我們還可以做朋友。)

也許我配不上你。	**Maybe I don´t deserve you.**
我們兩個不配。	**We don´t match each other.** A: If only we could become a couple. (如果我們能成爲情侶該有多好啊。) B: Don't read too much into it. We don't match each other. (別想太多了,我們兩個根本不配。)
你不是我喜歡的類型。	**You are not my type.**
我已經有男朋友了。	**I already have a boyfriend.** A: Can I date you? (我可以約你嗎?) B: Sorry, I already have a boyfriend. (對不起,我已經有男朋友了。) 
我很抱歉必須拒絕你。	**I am sorry to turn you down.**
別傻了。	**Don´t be silly.** A: I can do anything for you. (我可以爲你做任何事情。) B: Don't be silly. (別傻了。)
我現在還不想談戀愛。	**I don´t want to be in love now.**
我祇想在此刻專注我的事業。	**I am just at a moment when I need to focus on my career.** A: Why can't you accept me? (你爲什麽不能接受我呢?) B: It's just that the time isn't right. I am just at a moment when I need to focus on my career. (我們相遇的不是時候,我祇想在此刻專注我的事業。)
我們兩個不來電。	**There is no chemistry between us.**
你很好,但不是我心目中的女孩/男孩。	**You are good, but you are not the right girl/boy for me.** A: Am I not good enough? (是不是我不够好?) B: You are good, but you are not the right girl / boy for me. (你很好,但不是我心目中的女孩/男孩。)

其實你真的很好!

You are good enough actually.

也許有人比我更適合你。

There´s somebody better suited for you than me.

我們沒有緣分走在一起，那麼我們就各自尋找屬于自己的幸福吧。

If it is not our fate to walk in the same place, then we should respectively seek our own happiness.

我不想耽誤了你!

I don´t want to hold you up!

A: What do you think?
(你是怎麼想的呢？)
B: I don't want to hold you up!
(我不想耽誤了你！)

你在開玩笑吧!

You must be kidding.

A: I love you more than anything. (我愛你勝過一切。)
B: You must be kidding. (你在開玩笑吧！)

謝謝你的愛，但是我心裏已經有喜歡的人了。

Thanks for your love, but I have a guy to love.

A: I just want to say I love you.
(我衹想對你說，我愛你。)
B: Thanks for your love, but I have a guy to love.
(謝謝你的愛，但是我心裏已經有喜歡的人了。)

我沒有你想的那麼好。

I am not as good as you thought.

A: You are so perfect in my eyes.
(你在我眼裏是如此的完美。)
B: Maybe I am not as good as you thought.
(也許我并沒有你想象中的那麼好。)

祝福你早日找到自己的幸福。

Hope you´ll find your own love soon.

有些話還是不要說出來的好。

Some words shouldn´t be let out.

感情的事是不能勉強的。

Love can´t be forced.

約 會 Date

你今晚有空嗎? 回今天晚上有事嗎?	**Are you free tonight?** 回 **Do you have plans tonight?** A: Are you free tonight? (你今晚有空嗎?) B: Yes. Why? (有空,怎麽啦?) 注解 free“空閑的”。
今晚你能和我約會嗎?	**Do you want to go out with me tonight?** A: Do you want to go out with me tonight. (今晚你能和我約會嗎?) B: Yes, I do. But I need to finish my work first. (可以啊,但是我得先完成我手上的工作。) 注解 go out 并不一定就是“約會”,但是如果 go out 的後面直接跟 with me 的話,就一定是“約會”了。
今晚出去吧。	**Let´s go out tonight.** A: Let's go out tonight. (今晚出去吧。) B: Sorry, I'm already engaged this evening. (不好意思,我今晚已經有約了。) 
要是晚上有空,我們出去走走行嗎?	**If you´re free, why don´t we go out tonight?** A: If you're free, why don't we go out tonight? (要是晚上有空,我們出去走走行嗎?) B: Sounds great! (聽起來不錯。)
願意和我一起去看電影嗎?	**Would you like to go to the movies with me?** A: Would you like to go to the movies with me? (願意和我一起去看電影嗎?) B: Yeah, I'd love to. (當然,我很樂意。)
我們喝點茶什麽的吧。	**Let´s have tea or something.**
我們喝點什麽吧。	**Let´s have something to drink.**
能陪陪我嗎?	**Please keep me company for a while.** 注解 keep me company“和我在一起”、“交往”、“親近”。
我想請你看演出。	**I´d like to invite you to a show.**

今晚我們去吃自助餐怎麼樣?	**Should we go for a buffet tonight?** A: Should we go for a buffet tonight? (今晚我們去吃自助餐怎麼樣?) B: Good idea. (好主意。)
我能和你約會嗎?	**May I ask you out?** 同 **Would you go on a date with me?** 注解 ask out"約會"。go on a date with"約會"、"拍拖"。
在哪兒見面?	**Where do you want to meet?** A: Where do you want to meet? (在哪兒見面?) B: Any place you want. (你覺得哪兒合適就在哪兒。)
我們幾點見面?	**What time should we meet?** A: What time should we meet? (我們幾點見面?) B: How about nine? (9點怎麼樣?)
咖啡聽起來不錯, 你覺得怎麼樣?	**A cup of coffee sounds good, doesn´t it?** A: A cup of coffee sounds good,doesn't it? (咖啡聽起來不錯,你覺得怎麼樣?) B: Yes, but I think I'll have orange juice first. (不錯,不過我還是想喝點橙汁。) 
你想喝點什麼?	**Would you like anything to drink?** A: Would you like anything to drink? (你想喝點什麼?) B: I feel like having a coke. (我想喝可樂。)
我們先去購物中心,然後吃飯,最後去看電影。你覺得怎麼樣?	**First we go to the plaza, and then we can have dinner, then the movie. Is that ok with you?** A: First we go to the plaza, and then we can have dinner, then the movie. Is that ok with you? (我們先去購物中心,然後吃飯,最後去看電影。你覺得怎麼樣?) B: Okey-Dokey. (沒問題。)

● 分 手 Break Up

我想我們應該當好朋友就好了。	**I think we should just be friends.**

我們分手吧。	**Let´s break up.** A: Let's break up. (我們分手吧。) B: Ok, have a good break-up. (好,讓我們有個美好的分手。)
我厭倦了。	**I´m fed up.** A: Can you give me a chance, please? (你能再給我一次機會嗎?) B: I'm fed up. (我已經厭倦了。) 
我不願再見到你!	**I don´t want to see your face!**
我討厭你!	**I hate you!**
你怎麼回事?	**What´s wrong with you?**
你真讓我惡心!	**You make me sick!**
我没有安全感。	**I am insecure.** A: Why did you break it off with me? (你爲什麼要和我分手?) B: Because I am insecure. (因爲我没有安全感。)
我對你還有感情。	**I still have feelings for you.** A: I still have feelings for you. (我對你還有感情。) B: Feelings can't go forever, but you can. (感情是不會永遠消失的,但是你可以永遠消失。)
我希望最終我們能化解彼此之間的分歧然後重新合好。	**I hope we can finally work out our differences and get back together.** 注解 work out the differences "化解分歧", get back together "重新回到愛人的身邊。"
我已經另結新歡了。	**I´ve met someone else.** A: I've met someone else. (我已經另結新歡了。) B: How dare you! (你好大的膽子。)
我們都各自成長了。	**We´ve grown apart.**

我不再愛你了。	**I just don´t love you anymore.** A: I love you very much. (我很愛很愛你。) B: But I just don't love you anymore. (但是我已經不再愛你了。)
我們的感情真的行不通。	**It´s really not working.** A: Is there any chance of us starting over again? (我們還有機會重新來過嗎?) B: It's really not working. (我們的感情真的行不通。)
我們之間的愛情魔力已經不見了。	**The magic´s gone from our relationship.**
不是你的問題，是我的問題。	**It´s not you, it´s me.** A: Is there anything else I've done wrong? (是不是我做錯了什麼?) B: It's not you, it's me. (不是你的問題,是我的問題。)
我真的配不上你。	**You´re really too good for me.** A: You're really too good for me. (我真的配不上你。) B: It is an excuse. (這是借口。)
反正你也不是真的很愛我。	**You don´t really love me anyway.**
讓我們好聚好散吧，可以嗎?	**Let´s put a happy ending to it, ok?** A: Let's put a happy ending to it, ok? (讓我們好聚好散吧,可以嗎?) B: I respect your choice. (我尊重你的選擇。)
我真的不想被綁住。	**I really don´t want to be tied down.** A: I really don't want to be tied down. (我真的不想被綁住。) B: Ok, you are free. (好吧,你自由了。)
你會過得比我更好!	**You will be better off than me.**
我并不後悔我們的過去!	**I don´t regret our past.**

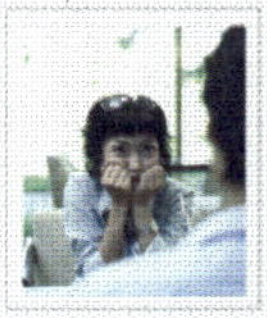

婚 姻 Marriage

結 婚 Getting Married

請嫁給我吧！

Please marry me!

A: Please marry me! (請嫁給我吧！)
B: Honey, please give me some time.
(親愛的，請給我一點時間。)

你願意嫁給我嗎?

Will you marry me?

A: Will you marry me? (你願意嫁給我嗎？)
B: Yes, I do. (我願意。)

我要你做我妻子。

I want you to be my wife.

A: I want you to be my wife. (我要你做我妻子。)
B: I love you but I can't marry you.
(我愛你但我不能和你結婚。)

我想和你共度餘生。

I want to spend the rest of my life with you.

我們什麼時候結婚?

When will we get married?

A: When will we get married? (我們什麼時候結婚？)
B: I have no intention of marrying yet.
(我還沒有結婚的打算。)

我還不想結婚。

I don´t want to get married yet.

A: I don't want to get married yet. (我還不想結婚。)
B: Are you serious? (你是説真的嗎？)

我還沒有做好結婚的準備。

I´m not ready to get married.

A: I'm not ready to get married.
(我還沒有做好結婚的準備。)
B: When will you be ready? (你什麼時候才做好準備？)

我想安定下來了。

I want to settle down.

你結婚了嗎?	**Are you married?** A: Are you married? (你結婚了嗎？) B: Not yet. I enjoy single life more. (還沒。我比較喜歡單身生活。)
你什麼時候結婚的?	**When did you get married?** A: When did you get married? (你什麼時候結婚的？) B: I've been married for three years. (我結婚 3 年了。)
我去年訂婚了。	**I got engaged last year.**
我是奉子成婚的。	**I got married because I was pregnant.** A: Your marriage was sudden. (你結婚結得太突然了。) B: I got married because I was pregnant. (我是奉子成婚的。)
我們倉促結了婚。	**We rushed into marriage.** A: We rushed into marriage. (我們倉促結了婚。) B: A shotgun marriage? (奉子成婚嗎？) 注解 shotgun marriage 是奉子成婚的意思。
我後悔結婚了。	**I regret getting married.** A: I regret getting married. (我後悔結婚了。) B: Aren't you enjoying your married life? (您現在不享受婚後的生活嗎？)
我覺得很幸福。	**I feel very happy.** A: How's your married life? (婚後生活如何？) B: I feel very happy. (我覺得很幸福。)
你們很配。	**You are a love match.**
我很遲才結婚。	**I got married late in life.** A: I got married late in life. (我很遲才結婚。) B: It's good to marry late. (晚婚是好事。)
我不同意你跟他結婚。	**I don´t approve of your getting married with him.**

她背着父母跟我結婚。

She married me without the knowledge of her parents.

A: She married me without the knowledge of her parents.
(她背着父母跟我結婚。)
B: She must love you so much.
(她一定很愛你。)

我們一畢業就結婚了。

We got married as soon as we graduated.

你想過要試婚嗎?

Have you thought about trial marriage?

A: Have you thought about trial marriage? (你想過要試婚嗎?)
B: I think it's unnecessary. (我覺得沒必要。)

我希望有一天可以跟他結婚。

I hope I can marry him one day.

A: I hope I can marry him one day.
(我希望有一天可以跟他結婚。)
B: You will. (你會的。)

我要娶她嗎?

Should I marry her?

A: Should I marry her? (我要娶她嗎?)
B: Do you love her? (你愛她嗎?)

我决定結婚了。

I decided to get married.

A: I decided to get married. (我决定結婚了。)
B: Really? Congratulations! (真的嗎? 恭喜你!)

你們要舉行婚禮嗎?

Are you going to hold a wedding?

A: Are you going to hold a wedding?
(你們要舉行婚禮嗎?)
B: Yes, it's in preparation. (要,正在準備。)

杰克和我下個月舉行婚禮。

Jack and I will hold a wedding next month.

A: Jack and I will hold a wedding next month. Will you come? (杰克和我下個月舉行婚禮。你會來吧?)
B: Of course. (當然。)

聽說你要結婚了,恭喜!

I heard that you´re getting married. Congratulations.

我們在教堂舉行婚禮。	**We married in church.**
在你新婚之際致以最美好的祝願。	**Best wishes on your marriage.**
謹賀你們締結良緣。	**Every good wish on your marriage.**
恭賀你喜結良緣。	**Congratulations on your marriage.**
祝你新婚快樂!	**I wish you a happy wedding!**
希望你婚後生活事事順心。	**I hope everything goes well with your married life.**
恭喜，祝你們有個美好的蜜月。	**Congratulations and have a wonderful honeymoon.**
你準備去哪度蜜月?	**Where are you going on your honeymoon?** A: Where are you going on your honeymoon? (你準備去哪度蜜月？) B: China. (中國。)
我們正在蜜月旅行。	**We are on the honeymoon trip.** A: We are on the honeymoon trip. (我們正在蜜月旅行。) B: Have a good trip! (旅途愉快！)
我倆將去巴塞羅那度蜜月。	**We will honeymoon in Barcelona.** A: We will honeymoon in Barcelona. (我倆將去巴塞羅那度蜜月。) B: Barcelona is a good place! (巴塞羅那，好地方！)
什麼時候去度蜜月?	**When will you go for honeymoon?** A: When will you go for honeymoon? (什麼時候去度蜜月？) B: After the wedding. (婚禮後就去。)
我們邀請了一百多個客人來參加婚宴。	**We invited more than 100 guests for our wedding party.**

你的婚戒很漂亮。	**Your wedding ring looks beautiful.**
我自己做的婚紗。	**I made the wedding gown myself.** A: What a wonderful wedding gown! (多美的婚紗啊!) B: I made the wedding gown myself. (我自己做的婚紗。)
你和你老公是怎麼認識的?	**How did you meet your husband?** A: How did you meet your husband? (你和你老公是怎麼認識的?) B: We were neighbors. (我們是鄰居。)

你老公怎麼向你求婚的?	**How did your husband propose to you?** A: How did your husband propose to you? (你老公怎麼向你求婚的?) B: He proposed to me when we traveled in a jewelry store. (我們一起去旅行的時候,在一家珠寶店他向我求婚了。)

離 婚 Divorce

婚姻生活真是讓人沮喪。	**Married life is very frustrating.** A: Married life is very frustrating. (婚姻生活真是讓人沮喪。) B: Why do you say that? (爲什麼這麼説?)
我不喜歡婚姻生活。	**I don´t like my wedlock.** A: I don't like my wedlock. (我不喜歡婚姻生活。) B: Why did you get married? (那你怎麼結婚了?)
我一點兒也不喜歡婚後生活。	**I don´t enjoy my married life at all.** A: I don't enjoy my married life at all. (我一點兒也不喜歡婚後生活。) B: Do you have any troubles? (有什麼困擾嗎?)
婚姻是愛情的墳墓。	**Marriage is the grave of love.** A: Marriage is the grave of love. (婚姻是愛情的墳墓。) B: That's what I think all the time. (我一直這麼認爲。)

我們的婚姻以離婚收場。

Our marriage ended in divorce.

A: Our marriage ended in divorce.
(我們的婚姻以離婚收場。)
B: Unbelievable. (真令人難以相信。)

我們的婚姻生活很短暫而且是吵吵鬧鬧的。

Our married life was short and tempestuous.

A: Our married life was short and tempestuous.
(我們的婚姻生活很短暫而且是吵吵鬧鬧的。)
B: Did you get along well before marriage?
(你們婚前相處得好嗎？)

我的婚姻破裂了。

My marriage was washed up.

A: You don't look well. What's up?
(你看起來不太好。怎麼了？)
B: My marriage was washed up. (我的婚姻破裂了。)

你後悔結婚嗎?

Do you regret getting married?

A: Do you regret getting married? (你後悔結婚嗎？)
B: No. After all, I knew I was not suitable for marriage.
(不後悔。畢竟我知道了自己不適合結婚。)

我離婚 1 年了。

I´ve been divorced for one year.

A: When did you get divorced? (你什麼時候離婚的？)
B: I've been divorced for one year. (我離婚 1 年了。)

他同意離婚了。

He consented to the divorce.

A: He consented to the divorce. (他同意離婚了。)
B: What a fool he was. (他真是個傻瓜。)

我們離婚了。

We got divorced.

A: We got divorced. (我們離婚了。)
B: For what? (爲什麼？)

離婚以後，我獲得了孩子的監護權。

After divorce, I got custody of the children.

A: After divorce, I got custody of the children.
(離婚以後，我獲得了孩子的監護權。)
B: It seems that you get along well with your children.
(你跟孩子們的關系看起來不錯。)

我已向法院申請離婚。	**I have filed a petition for divorce.** A: I have filed a petition for divorce. (我已向法院申請離婚。) B: Do you really want to split up? (你真的想離婚嗎?)
我爲了離婚之事而煩悶。	**I agonized over the divorce.** A: What's eating you? (你爲什麼悶悶不樂?) B: I agonized over the divorce. (我爲了離婚之事而煩悶。)
我有充分的理由跟你離婚。	**I have adequate grounds for a divorce.**  A: Why do you want to get divorce? (爲什麼要跟我離婚?) B: I have adequate grounds for a divorce. (我有充分的理由跟你離婚。)
離婚後，我簡直是身心都崩潰了。	**After divorce I seemed to be coming apart at the seams.** A: How's it going? (最近怎樣?) B: After divorce I seemed to be coming apart at the seams. (離婚後,我簡直是身心都崩潰了。)
由于我已經離婚了，我覺得自由自在。	**Now that I´ve got my divorce, I feel as free as a bird.** A: Now that I've got my divorce, I feel as free as a bird. (由于我已經離婚了,我覺得自由自在。) B: So you like your present life? (你喜歡現在的生活咯?)
他離婚後不久又匆忙結婚了。	**He got divorced and rushed head first into another marriage.** A: How's he? (他最近怎樣?) B: Not bad. He got divorced and rushed head first into another marriage. (不錯啊! 他離婚後不久又匆忙結婚了。)
我們決定分居。	**We decide to live apart.** A: How do you decide? (你們怎麼決定?) B: We decide to live apart. (我們決定分居。)

她對離婚看得很開。	**She has a liberal attitude to divorce.** A: Is she all right? (她還好吧？) B: Don't worry. She has a liberal attitude to divorce. (放心。她對離婚看得很開。)
我最終從離婚的創傷中恢復了。	**I finally got over the divorce.** A: I finally got over the divorce. (我最終從離婚的創傷中恢復了。) B: You're very strong. (你很堅强。)
我和妻子分居了。	**My wife and I are separated.** A: My wife and I are separated. (我和妻子分居了。) B: What happened to you? (發生什麼事了？)
我們經常吵架。	**We fight a lot.** A: We fight a lot. I can't bear it. (我們經常吵架。我受不了了。) B: I can't bear it, too. (我也受不了了。)
我老婆有外遇。	**My wife is having an affair.** A: My wife is having an affair. (我老婆有外遇。) B: What are you going to do? (你打算怎麼辦？)
我懷疑我老公有外遇。	**I suspect my husband of running around.** A: I suspect my husband of running around. (我懷疑我老公有外遇。) B: Calm dowm to make it clear. (冷静，先把事情弄清楚。)
我感到和你在一起很累。	**I find you exhausting to be with.** A: I find you exhausting to be with. (我感到和你在一起很累。) B: Why do you feel like that way? (為什麼你會這樣覺得？) 
我對你没感覺了。	**I have no feelings for you anymore.** A: Don't you love me any more? (你不再愛我了嗎？) B: I have no feelings for you anymore. (我對你没感覺了。)

聊 天 Chat

社 會 About Society

我沒有加入任何政黨。

I didn´t join any political party.

A: What political party do you belong to?
(你是哪個政黨的成員?)

B: I didn't join any political party.
(我沒有加入任何政黨。)

許多人熱衷政治。

Many people crave politics.

政局會影響經濟。

The political situation will influence the economy.

我從未對政治活動感興趣。

Politics has never interested me.

你今年投票了嗎?

Did you vote this year?

你家附近的治安好嗎?

Is it safe around your neighborhood?

A: Is it safe around your neighborhood?
(你家附近治安好嗎?)

B: Not bad. (還行。)

治安越來越差了。

Public security is getting worse and worse.

A: Yesterday I was robbed. (我昨天被搶了。)

B: Public security is getting worse and worse.
(治安越來越差了。)

貧富差距越來越大。

The gap between the rich and the poor is getting wider and wider.

A: The gap between the rich and the poor is getting wider and wider. (貧富差距越來越大。)

B: Is the government trying to solve the problem?
(政府有在想辦法解决這個問題嗎?)

我不是有錢人，但我很快樂。

I´m not rich, but I´m happy.

A: I'm not rich, but I'm happy.
(我不是有錢人，但我很快樂。)
B: Happy is important. (快樂很重要。)

你羨慕有錢人嗎?

Do you envy the rich?

A: Do you envy the rich? (你羨慕有錢人嗎？)
B: No. Being rich does not mean being happy.
(不，有錢也不一定快樂。)

很多人買不起房子。

Many people cannot afford to buy an apartment.

A: Many people cannot afford to buy an apartment.
(很多人買不起房子。)
B: The apartments are too expensive to afford.
(房子已經貴到讓人買不起了。)

不景氣使得許多人失業。

The recession threw many people out of work.

A: The recession threw many people out of work.
(不景氣使得許多人失業。)
B: Unemployment poses many problems.
(失業會帶來許多問題。)

你擔心失業嗎?

Do you worry about unemployment?

A: Do you worry about unemployment?
(你擔心失業嗎？)
B: It's useless to worry. (擔心也沒用。)

有些人失業後選擇自己創業。

Some people choose to start their own businesses after becoming unemployed.

你對加班有什麼看法?

How do you feel about overtime work?

A: How do you feel about overtime work?
(你對加班有什麼看法？)
B: Who likes to work overtime? (有誰喜歡加班呢？)

許多學生吸毒。

Many students shoot up.

A: Many students shoot up. (許多學生吸毒。)
B: The use of narcotics by teenagers is a big problem.
(少年吸食毒品是一個大問題。)

許多年輕人吸毒尋求刺激。	**Many young people are taking drugs to turn on.** A: She was kicked out of her university for taking drugs. (她因吸毒而被大學開除。) B: Many young people are taking drugs to turn on. (許多年輕人吸毒尋求刺激。)
吸毒成癮的人常常產生幻覺。	**Drug addicts often hallucinate.**
她在吸毒後變得完全失去了理性。	**After taking the drug she became completely irrational.**
許多上班族不得不加班。	**Many office workers have to work overtime.**
全職上班族平均開始工作的時間是上午 10 點，而下午 3 點半左右就開始懈怠了。	**The average full–time office worker doesn´t even start doing real work until 10:00am and begins to wind down around 3:30pm.**
一項調查顯示，三分之一的上班族早上寧願多睡幾分鐘，也不願起床吃早餐。	**According to a survey, one–third of office workers would rather grab a few minutes extra sleep than breakfast.** 
我們經常聽說有人跳槽。	**We often hear about people making radical career changes.** A: We often hear about people making radical career changes. (我們經常聽說有人跳槽。) B: Job-hopping is common in big cities. (在大城市跳槽是常事。)
毫無疑問，跳槽有優點也有缺點。	**There is no doubt that job –hopping has its drawbacks as well as merits.** A: Could job-hopping be good for our career? (跳槽對我們的職業生涯有益嗎？) B: There is no doubt that job-hopping has its drawbacks as well as merits. (毫無疑問，跳槽有優點也有缺點。)

你考慮過跳槽嗎?	**Are you thinking of jumping ship?**
我不知道我的孩子在想什麼。	**I don´t know what my child is thinking.** A: I don't know what my child is thinking. (我不知道我的孩子在想什麼。) B: How often do you chat? (你們多久聊一次天？)
怎樣才能和孩子溝通?	**How can I communicate with my child?** A: How can I communicate with my child? (怎樣才能和孩子溝通？) B: First of all, you should respect your child. (首先你要尊重你的孩子。)
家庭是青少年問題的起因。	**Family is the origin of the juvenile problem.**
青少年需要家長的關心。	**Youth need care from parents.** A: Youth need care from parents. (青少年需要家長的關心。) B: But many parents are too busy to care for their children. (可是很多家長都沒時間關心孩子。)
一些青少年對毒品沒有抵抗力。	**Some juveniles don´t have any resistance to drugs.**
青少年時的朋友影響很大。	**The friends of one´s youth are very influential.**

● 生 活 About Life

今天不下雨。	**It´s not raining today.** A: It's not raining today. (今天不下雨。) B: The game will be held on time. (比賽如期舉行。)
明天有雷暴雨。	**A heavy thunderstorm tomorrow.** A: What will the weather be like tomorrow? (明天的天氣怎樣?) B: A heavy thunderstorm tomorrow. (明天有雷暴雨。)

天氣真好!	**What a fine day!** A: What a fine day! (天氣真好!) B: It's finally clearing up. (總算放晴了。)
光打雷不下雨。	**It thundered, but no rain fell.**
天氣預報經常不準確。	**The weather forecast is often inaccurate.**
天氣總算不壞。	**On the whole the weather is not bad.**
今年夏天不太熱。	**It´s not very hot this summer.**
你喜歡哪個季節?	**Which season do you like?** A: Which season do you like? (你喜歡哪個季節?) B: Summer. I can enjoy a lot of ice cream. (夏天。我可以吃好多的冰激凌。)
我還没見過雪。	**I haven´t seen snow.** A: I haven't seen snow. (我還没見過雪。) B: I can't believe it. (不是吧?)
習慣這裏的天氣嗎?	**Are you ok with the weather here?**
没有風,好熱。	**It´s windless and hot.**
你喜歡旅游嗎?	**Do you like traveling?** A: Do you like traveling? (你喜歡旅游嗎?) B: Yeah. I go traveling once a year at least. (喜歡,每年至少去一次旅游。)
你喜歡去什麼地方旅游?	**Where do you like to travel?** A: Where do you like to travel? (你喜歡去什麼地方旅游?) B: I like to go to Europe. I like the buildings there. (我喜歡去歐洲,喜歡那裏的建築。)
我會在網上查找一些相關信息。	**I search for relevant information online.**

你一個人去嗎?	**You go alone?** A: You go alone? (你一個人去嗎?) B: It depends. (看情况。)
你喜歡跟團還是自助游?	**Do you prefer going with travel groups or going by yourself?** A: Do you prefer going with travel groups or going by yourself? (你喜歡跟團還是自助游?) B: I prefer going by myself. (我比較喜歡自助游。)
這次的旅行花了多少錢?	**How much did you pay for this trip?** A: How much did you pay for this trip? (這次旅行花了多少錢?) B: Eight hundred dollars. (800 美元。)
你去過什麼地方?	**Where have you been?** A: Where have you been? (你去過什麼地方?) B: Canada and Africa. (加拿大和非洲。)
這次旅行去多長時間?	**How long will you travel this time?** A: How long will you travel this time? (這次旅行去多長時間?) B: Half a month. (半個月。)
七八月是旅游旺季。	**July and August are the peak seasons of tourism.** A: July and August are the peak seasons of tourism. (七八月是旅游旺季。) B: Well, I'll change my time. (那我換個時間去吧。)
我經常頭痛。	**I often have a headache.** A: I often have a headache. (我經常頭痛。) B: Take care of yourself. (注意身體啊!)
有去看醫生嗎?	**Have you gone to the doctor?** A: Have you gone to the doctor? (有去看醫生嗎?) B: Yeah. The doctor asked me to do more exercise. (有。醫生叫我多做運動。)

最近老是失眠。	**Recently I couldn´t fall asleep.** A: You look sleepy. (你看起來沒什麼精神。) B: Recently I couldn't fall asleep. (最近老是失眠。)
我一年做一次身體檢查。	**I get a physical examination yearly.** A: Do you get body check regularly? (你定期檢查身體嗎？) B: I get a physical examination yearly. (我一年做一次身體檢查。) 
我工作很忙所以很累。	**My work is very busy so that I´m very tired.** A: You've been tired, haven't you? (你最近是不是很累？) B: My work is very busy so that I'm very tired. (我工作很忙所以很累。)
我盡量讓自己的生活變得規律。	**I´m trying to keep my lifestyle in a more regular pattern.** A: I'm trying to keep my lifestyle in a more regular pattern. (我盡量讓自己的生活變得規律。) B: Living a regular life is conducive to good health. (生活規律有益身體健康。)
你還是經常熬夜嗎?	**Do you still stay up often?** A: Do you still stay up often? (你還是經常熬夜嗎？) B: No. I go to bed before midnight. (沒有，我晚上 12 點前就睡覺了。)
你吸烟嗎?	**Do you smoke?** A: Do you smoke? (你吸烟嗎？) B: I never smoke. (我從不吸烟。)
我覺得戒烟很不容易。	**I find it difficult to stop smoking.** A: You should stop smoking. (你應該戒烟。) B: Well, I find it difficult to stop smoking. (可是我覺得戒烟很不容易。)
我的孩子總是不喜歡吃蔬菜。	**My child always turn up his nose at vegetables.**

昨晚的酒還没醒。	**I have a hangover.** A: I have a hangover. (昨晚的酒還没醒。) B: You drank too much. (你喝太多了。)
我已經習慣在外面吃飯了。	**I am used to eating out all the time.** A: Do you cook your own food? (你自己做飯嗎？) B: I am used to eating out all the time. (我已經習慣在外面吃飯了。)
多吃水果和蔬菜，定期鍛煉會改善我們的健康狀况。	**More fruits and vegetables and regular exercises will improve our health.**
你應該多吃一些水果。	**You should eat some fruit more.** A: You should eat some fruit more. (你應該多吃一些水果。) B: I always forget to eat. (我總是不記得吃。)
吃當地的水果更健康。	**Eating local fruits is healthier.** A: Eating local fruits is healthier. (吃當地的水果更健康。) B: But I don't like to eat local fruits. (可當地的水果我都不喜歡吃。)

● 雜七雜八 Odds and Ends

我每天鍛煉減肥。	**I have been doing exercises to lose weight every day.** A: I have been taking exercises to lose weight every day. (我每天鍛煉減肥。) B: Exercise is a sure way of losing weight. (運動是減肥的可靠辦法。)
我讓自己挨餓來減肥。	**I´m starving myself, trying to lose weight.** A: Have you ever heard of eating gruel to lose weight? (你有没有聽説過吃稀飯減肥的?) B: No. I'm starving myself, trying to lose weight. (没有。我讓自己挨餓來減肥。)

我變胖了。	**I gain weight.** A: I gain weight. (我變胖了。) B: But you don't look fat. (但你看起來不胖。)
夏天快到了,該減肥了。	**Summer is coming, I have to lose weight.** A: Summer is coming, I have to lose weight. (夏天快到了,該減肥了。) B: Wish you success reducing weight! (祝你減肥成功!)
胖了穿衣服就不好看了。	**You don´t look good in the clothes once you gain weight.** A: You don't look good in the clothes once you gain weight. (胖了穿衣服就不好看了。) B: So I am trying to lose weight now. (所以我正在減肥。)
減肥藥有用嗎?	**Are slimming pills effective?** A: Are slimming pills effective? (減肥藥有用嗎?) B: It is said that you'll gain weight after stop taking the pills. (據説停藥後會反彈。)
你還吃減肥藥嗎?	**Are you still using the slimming pills?** A: Are you still using the slimming pills? (你還在吃減肥藥嗎?) B: No. I jog every morning. (没吃了。我現在每天早上跑步。) 
爲何不試試運動來減肥?	**Why not try exercising to lose weight?** A: Why not try exercising to lose weight? (爲何不試試運動來減肥?) B: Exercise is tiring to me. (運動太累人了。)
要減肥成功,必須持之以恒。	**To succeed in losing weight, you have to keep working hard to meet your goal.** A: To succeed in losing weight, you have to keep working hard to meet your goal. (要減肥成功,必須持之以恒。) B: I'll stick to that. (我會堅持的。)

你怎麼減肥?	**What do you do to lose weight?** A: What do you do to lose weight? (你怎麼減肥？) B: Take slimming pills. (吃減肥藥。)
爲了減肥,我不吃糖。	**In order to lose weight, I refrain from eating candy.** A: In order to lose weight, I refrain from eating candy. (爲了減肥,我不吃糖。) B: How long have you kept on? (你堅持多久了？)
我不想吃蛋糕,我正在減肥。	**I don´t want any cake, I´m slimming.** A: Would you like some cake? (你要吃蛋糕嗎？) B: I don't want any cake, I'm slimming. (我不想吃蛋糕，我正在減肥。)
有氧運動是女性減肥的最佳方式。	**Aerobic exercise is the optimal method for women to lose weight.** A: Aerobic exercise is the optimal method for women to lose weight. (有氧運動是女性減肥的最佳方式。) B: What is aerobic exercise? (哪些是有氧運動？)
慢跑是一項減肥的好運動。	**Jogging is a good exercise to get slim.**
你覺得吃減肥食譜怎樣?	**What do you think of on a diet?** A: What do you think of on a diet? (你覺得吃減肥食譜怎樣？) B: This should be a healthy way to lose weight. (這個應該是健康的減肥方式。) 
爲了穿上那件衣服,我必須減肥。	**I must reduce to get into that dress.** A: I must reduce to get into that dress. (爲了穿上那件衣服,我必須減肥。) B: Come on. Don't give up easily. (加油,别輕易放弃。)
你瘦了好多啊!	**You have thinned down a lot!** A: You have thinned down a lot! (你瘦了好多啊！) B: I think there's room for me to lose a little weight. (我覺得還可以再瘦一點。)

我衹買名牌服裝。	**I only buy brand–name clothing.** A: Do you like to buy name brand items? (你喜歡買名牌嗎？) B: I only buy brand-name clothing. (我衹買名牌服裝。)
這牌子的衣服應該很好賣。	**This brand of clothes should sell well.** A: The design is unique. (設計真特別。) B: This brand of clothes should sell well. (這牌子的衣服應該很好賣。)
這件衣服是最新設計。	**This dress is the latest design.** A: The dress is so expensive. (這件衣服很貴。) B: This dress is the latest design. (這件衣服是最新設計。)
這是真的還是仿的?	**Is it real or an imitation?** A: Is it real or an imitation? (這是真的還是仿的？) B: How could I buy an imitation? (我怎麼會買仿的呢？)
這種衣服現在很時髦。	**This kind of dress is now in fashion.** A: This kind of dress is now in fashion. (這種衣服現在很時髦。) B: It can be seen everywhere. (到處都可以看到。)
你對衣服很挑剔。	**You are fastidious in your dress.** A: You are fastidious in your dress. (你對衣服很挑剔。) B: I trust in the quality of name brand. (我相信名牌的品質。)
你會分期付款買名牌嗎?	**Will you pay for name brand items by installments?** A: Will you pay for name brand items by installments? (你會分期付款買名牌嗎？) B: I will if I like it very much. (如果很喜歡的話，我會。)
你在哪兒買到那件東西?	**Where did you buy that thing?** A: Where did you buy that thing? (你在哪兒買到那件東西？) B: In the flea market. (跳蚤市場。)

你在網上買東西嗎?	**Do you shop online?** A: Do you shop online? (你在網上買東西嗎？) B: Yeah. Online shopping is very convenient. (買啊。網上買東西很方便。)
你想過去整形嗎?	**Have you thought of getting plastic surgery?**
你最想改變哪一個部位?	**Which part of your body would you like to change most?** A: Which part of your body would you like to change most? (你最想改變哪一個部位？) B: Eyes. (眼睛。) 
一些整形手術的費用很高。	**The prices of some plastic surgical operations are very expensive.**
有魚尾紋了,怎麼辦?	**What should I do about crow´s feet?**
我想拉皮。	**I want to get face–lifts.**
我姐姐前幾天去割雙眼皮了。	**My sister had a double eyelid operation a few days ago.**
夏天我的皮膚又油又黏。	**In summer, my skin is always oily sticky.**
無聊的時候我看八卦新聞。	**I read gossip magazine when I feel bored.** A: Do you like to read gossip magazine? (你喜歡看八卦雜志嗎？) B: I read gossip magazine when I feel bored. (無聊的時候我看八卦新聞。)
你相信八卦雜志寫的嗎?	**Do you believe the articles of gossip magazine?** A: Do you believe the articles of gossip magazine? (你相信八卦雜志寫的嗎？) B: I don't believe. Much gossip is bullshit. (不相信。很多新聞都是胡扯的。)

拜 訪 Visit

歡迎！請進。	**Welcome! Come in, please.** A: Welcome! Come in, please. (歡迎！請進。) B: Sorry for bothering you. (打擾了。)
很高興你能來。	**I´m so glad that you could come.** A: Thank you for your invitation. (謝謝你的邀請。) B: I'm so glad that you could come. (很高興你能來。)
你來得真早。	**You came so early.** A: You came so early. (你來得真早。) B: I was afraid that there would be heavy traffic, so I left a little earlier. (我擔心會塞車，所以提早出門了。)
你怎麽來的？	**How did you get here?** A: How did you get here? (你怎麽來的？) B: I took a cab. (我坐計程車來的。)
這是一點小禮物。	**This is a small gift.** A: This is a small gift. (這是一點小禮物。) B: Thanks for your gift. You're so kind. (謝謝你的禮物，你太客氣了。) 
這套公寓不錯。	**This apartment looks nice.** A: This apartment looks nice. (這套公寓不錯。) B: Thank you. I have been living here for 10 years. (謝謝。我已經在這裏住了 10 年了。)
小區環境很好。	**The plot environment is good.**
你的房子的布置很有品味。	**Your house is tastefully laid out.**
請坐。	**Please sit down.**

當自己家一樣。	**Make yourself at home.**
你要喝什麼?	**What would you like to drink?** A: What would you like to drink? (你要喝什麼?) B: Tea, please. (茶,謝謝。)
你要吃什麼,我幫你拿。	**Let me help you get something you want to eat.** A: Let me help you get something you want to eat. (你要吃什麼,我幫你拿。) B: I'll help myself. You don't need to take care of me. (我自己來,你別忙。)
嘗嘗我的拿手菜。	**Give a try at my special dish.** A: Give a try at my special dish. (嘗嘗我的拿手菜。) B: Wow! Every dish looks very delicious. (哇! 每道菜看起來都很好吃。)
吃甜點嗎?	**Would you like some desserts?**
有沒有吃飽?	**Are you full?** A: Are you full? (有沒有吃飽?) B: Yes, I am full, thanks. (吃飽了,謝謝!)
吃點水果。	**Help yourselves to the fruit.**
我想用一下洗手間。	**I need to use the restroom.**
我差不多該回去了。	**It´s about time to leave.**
歡迎隨時來玩。	**Drop in anytime.** 回 **Come by anytime. You are always welcome to our house.**
有沒有東西忘了拿?	**Have you forgotten anything?**
我送你們出去。	**I´ll walk out with you.**
路上小心。	**Take care.**

報 警 Police Report

● 信用卡丟失 Loss of Credit Card

我打電話報警，我的信用卡丟了。	I´m calling to report a missing credit card.
信用卡號碼是多少，小姐?	What´s the card number, miss?
您說您的信用卡是丟失還是被偷了?	Did you say your card was lost or stolen?
我去試衣室試衣時，把錢包放在百貨公司的櫃臺上了。	I left my purse on the counter in the department store while I went to the fitting room to try the dress on.
您什麼時候發現信用卡被偷了呢?	When did you discover it was stolen?
我去付錢的時候才發現。	I didn´t discover that until I went to pay.
可能現在就有人正用我的信用卡買東西呢。	Someone may be charging things to my credit card at moment.
我們一弄清您的信用卡號碼，祇要在 30 秒鐘之內，您的信用卡就會在世界各地失效。	Once we get your card number, your card will be invalidated all over the world within 30 seconds simply. 
你這麼說我就放心了。	I´m so relieved to hear that.

● 搶 劫 Robbery

我想要報案。	I want to report a crime.

你的姓名、地址、電話?	**What´s your name, address, and telephone number?**
你要報什麽案?	**What do you want to report?**
店內偷竊。	**Shoplifting.**
請描述歹徒相貌特徵。	**Please describe the suspect.** 注解 Height 身高;Weight 體重;Sex 性别;Skin Color 膚色;Dress 衣着;Significance 特徵。
有没有看到歹徒用的車輛?	**Did you see suspect´s vehicle?** 注解 Model 車型;Make 制造車廠;Plate Number 車牌號碼。
何時發生? 何地發生?	**When did it happen? Where did it happen?**
有没有目擊證人?	**Any witness?**
損失了什麽財物?	**What properties did you lose?**

● 盜 匪 Burglary

我家被偷了。	**My house has been burglarized.**
我睡覺時忘了鎖上窗户,一個竊賊從窗户鑽進來,把我們洗劫一空。	**I went to sleep and forgot to lock the window and a burglar came in the window and cleaned us out.**
我是説他把值錢的東西都偷走了包括錢、手表、電視、VCD、所有東西。	**I mean he took all valuables such as money, watches, TV, VCD.**
我的車子昨天晚上被偷了。	**My car was stolen last night.**
車子原來停在什麽地方呢?	**And where was it parked?**

先生，是哪一種車？	What kind of car is it, sir?
牌照號碼是 ABC123。	The license plate number is ABC123.
車子原來停在我家前面的車道上。	It was parked in my driveway in front of my house.
能不能告訴我大概什麽時間被偷的？	Can you tell me the time period when it was stolen?
防盜器響了，但是他們一定把它切斷了。	The car alarm went off, but they must´ve disengaged it.
我們一整夜都在這裏，您當時爲什麽不打電話來呢？	We´re open all night here. Why didn´t you call then?
我以爲是鬧鐘在響，所以看了看鐘，重新設定時間後，又睡了。	I thought it was my alarm clock, so I looked at the clock, reset it, and went back to sleep.

急救電話 Emergency Calls

九一一，您有什麽緊急情況？	911, what is your emergency?
有人心臟病發作，需要一部救護車。	Someone is having a heart attack. Please send an ambulance over.
我的鄰居家着火了。	There is a fire in my neighbor´s house.
緊急事故的位置及撥打緊急事故的號碼是什麽？	What is the location of emergency and number you are calling from?
緊急事故的地址是在 5 大道和麥迪森街的拐角。	The location is at the corner of 5th Ave and Madison Street.
救護車和警察大概 10 分鐘就能到達。	The ambulance and police should be there in about 5 minutes.

交通事故 Car Accident

我通報交通意外。	I am calling to report a car accident.
交通意外的地點是堅尼路及包裹街。	The intersections streets of the accident are Canal Street and Bowery.
有沒有人在此交通意外中嚴重受傷?	Anybody seriously injured in the traffic accident?
你的聯絡電話是什麼?	What is your contact number?
救護車及警察在 5 分鐘內會到達。	The ambulance and police officers should be there in 5 minutes.
您沒事兒吧?	Are you Ok? 同 Are you all right?
您受傷了嗎?	Are you hurt? 同 Are you injured?
你需要去醫院嗎?	Do you need to go to the hospital?
您要救護車嗎?	Do you need an ambulance?
能不能告訴我這兒發生了什麼事?	Can you tell me what happened here?
在車撞上您之前，您看見車了嗎?	Did you see the car before it hit you?
您開多快?	How fast were you going?
您是從哪個方向來的?	Which direction were you coming from?
您要往哪個方向去?	Which direction were you going?

您和前面車子的距離是多少?	How far were you from the car in front of you?
當時您在哪個車道行駛?	Which lane were you in?
您注意到紅燈了嗎?	Have you noticed the red light?
您移動過您的車嗎?	Have you moved your car?
請不要移動您的車輛。	Please do not move your vehicle.
請把您的車移到路邊。	Please move your vehicle to the side of the road.
我可以看您的保險及行車證嗎?	Can I see your insurance card and registration?
您有任何這次意外的證人嗎?	Do you have any witness for the accident?
雙方的總共損失少于$200,還需要填寫警察報告嗎?	Do you still want to file a police report since the damages is less than $200.00.
您的汽車保險可能會因爲您申報了警察報告而上升。	Your car insurance might go up once you file a police report.
我們需要對您進行酒精濃度測試?	We need to do blood alcohol level test on you.
這裏發送了撞車後逃命的事故。	There is a hit and run accident.
逃跑的車是黑色本田思威。	It is a black Honda CR-V.
48 小時後可以到 5 分局取事故報告。	The Police report will be ready for pick up at 5th Precinct in 48 hours.

Work
【工　作】

- 辦公室
- 客　户

辦公室 At the Office

你又遲到了。

You are late again.

A: You are late again. (你又遲到了！)

B: Traffic was too heavy today. (今天交通太擁擠了。)

我祇遲到了 5 分鐘。

I was only late by five minutes.

同 I was only five minutes late.

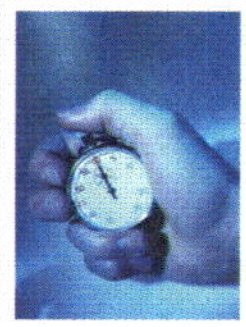

打出勤卡了嗎?

Did you punch in?

A: Did you punch in? (你打出勤卡了嗎?)

B: Oh, no. I forgot. (噢！不，我給忘了呢。)

讓我看看我的日程安排。

Let me check my schedule.

同 Let me look over my schedule.

Let me confirm my schedule.

A: Jane, can you finish the assignment this week?
(珍，你這個星期能完成任務嗎？)

B: I am not sure. Let me check my schedule.
(不太確定，讓我先看看我的日程安排。)

我有好多事要幹。

I've got so much to do.

同 I have many things to do.

A: Let's take a rest for a while. (我們先休息一會吧。)

B: No, I can't. I've got so much to do. (我不能休息，我有好多事情要幹。)

我非常忙。

I'm extremely busy.

A: Can you help me with my work? (你能幫我完成這項工作嗎？)

B: Sorry, I'm extremely busy. (對不起，我非常忙。)

我是個普通的公司職員。

I'm an ordinary office worker.

注解 ordinary“平凡，普通”。“男職員”、“女職員”均用 an office worker 表示。

我的時間安排很緊。	**I´m pressed for time.**
這工作不太費事。	**The work doesn´t need much effort.** **同 It´s an easy job.** A: The work doesn't need much effort. (這工作不太費事。) B: You are so lucky. (那你太幸運了。)
幹活別偷懶!	**Don´t neglect your duties!** A:Don't neglect your duties! (幹活別偷懶。) B: Okay. I won't. (好的,絕不偷懶。) 注解 neglect"不認真對待工作,不履行義務,馬馬虎虎的態度"。Duty"義務"。
請把這個訂在一起。	**Please staple these together.** 注解 stapler 是名詞,"訂書機"。staple 爲動詞,"訂在一起"。
打起精神來。	**Pull yourself together.** A: I am so tired. (我太累了。) B: Just put yourself together. (打起精神來!) 注解 pull oneself together"打起精神,振作起來"。
我犯了個很大的錯誤。	**I just made a big mistake.** A: I just made a big mistake. (我犯了個很大的錯誤。) B: Don't worry, it will be ok. (別擔心,沒事的。)
我們休息一會兒吧。	**Let´s take a break.**
快到午餐時間了。	**It´s almost lunchtime.** **同 It´s almost time for lunch.** A: I am too hungry to work. (我餓到無法工作了。) B: It's almost lunchtime. (快到午餐時間了。)
我們有 1 小時的午休時間。	**We take an hour lunch break.**
我們開始吧。	**Let´s get started.**

現在我不能放下這項工作。

I can´t leave this job at the moment.

A: I heard you'll have a business trip lately.
(聽說你最近要出差。)

B: Yes, but I can't leave this job at the moment.
(是的，問題是我現在不能放下這項工作。)

我太忙了，顧不上那麼瑣碎的事。

I´m too busy to bother with such details.

注解 detail“細小的，零碎的”。

這個計劃還得找人幫忙。

I need more help with the project.

A: I need more help with the project.
(這個計劃還得找人幫忙。)

B: Well, you can count on me. (那你可以找我呀。)

我的名字叫史蒂夫·桑德斯。

My name is Steve Saunders.

A: What is your name? (請問你怎麼稱呼？)

B: My name is Steve Saunders. (我的名字叫史蒂夫.桑德斯。)

我是新來的同事！

I am new here.

A: Hello! I am new here. (你好，我是新來的同事。)

B: I'll show you around. (我帶你熟悉一下環境吧！)

你能告訴我你的傳真號碼嗎？

Can you tell me your fax number?

您有預約嗎？

Do you have an appointment?

A: Do you have an appointment? (您有預約嗎？)

B: No, but I have something urgent to talk about with him. (沒有，但是我有非常緊急的事情要跟他說。)

我去看看他現在是否在辦公室。

I´ll see if he is available now.

A: I'd like to see Mr. Johnson, please.
(我想見約翰遜先生。)

B: Wait for a moment, I'll see if he is available now.
(請稍等片刻，我去看看他現在是否在辦公室。)

請您稍等片刻！

Wait for a moment, please!

給他電話，看看他現在能否發份傳真過來。	**Give him a call and see if he can send a fax now.**
有什麼能幫您的嗎?	**May I help you?** A: Good morning, miss. May I help you? (小姐，早上好！有什麼能幫您的嗎？) B: I'd like to see Mr. Smith, please. (我想見見史密斯先生。)
您需要給他留個口信嗎?	**Would you like to leave a message?** A: I'm sorry, Mr. Li is not here. Would you like to leave a message? (很抱歉，李先生不在，您需要給他留個口信嗎？) B: Yes, my name is Michael, and my phone number is 888-862-1018. (好的，我的名字叫米高，電話號碼是：888-862-1018。)
他應當已經收到我的傳真了。	**He should receive my fax.**
我猜是傳真機又沒紙了。	**I guess the fax machine is out of paper again.**
這是我的電子郵件地址。	**This is my email address.**
請盡快把細節用電子郵件傳給我。	**Please email me the details as soon as you can.**
我會在今天下午把資料傳真或寄電子郵件給你。	**I will either fax or email that information to you this afternoon.** A: I want to get it as soon as possible. (我想盡早拿到這份資料。) B: I will either fax or email that information to you this afternoon. (我會在今天下午把資料傳真或寄電子郵件給你。) 
收到價目表後，請以電子郵件或者傳真的方式確認。	**Please confirm receipt of the price list by email or fax.**

客　戶 About Customers

最近工作怎麼樣?	**How are things at the office lately?** A: How are things at the office lately? (最近工作怎麼樣?) B: Just awful. (不好　) 注解 lately,副詞,"近來,最近"的意思。
你們部門的人好像很能幹。	**The people in your department seem so capable.**
她很好相處。	**She is nice to be around.** A: How is your supervisor? (你們的主管人怎麼樣?) B: She is nice to be around. (她很好相處。)
盡管他還沒什麼經驗,但是個不錯的同事。	**Even though he´s still a bit green, he is a great coworker.**
每個人都有自己的長處和短處。	**Everybody has his / her strengths and weaknesses.**
與其他同事相比,有些同事比較難共事。	**Some coworkers are harder to work with than others.**
就這個提案,我有幾個不同的想法。	**I came up with different thoughts on this proposal.** A: Do you have any good idea? (你有什麼好主意嗎?) B: I came up with different thoughts on this proposal. (就這個提案,我有幾個不同的想法。) 
這個辦法可行。	**This is one possible solution.**
我們得想出一個解決這問題的辦法。	**We´ve got to come up with a way to solve this problem.**

你和同事的關系如何?	**Do you get along with your coworkers?** A: Do you get along with your coworkers? (你和同事的關系如何?) B: I get along pretty well with most of them. (我和他們大部分人處得都很不錯。) 注解 get along with... 意爲:與……和睦相處。
到我辦公室裏來談談。	**Come to my office and talk to me.** A: Mr. White, I have some suggestions. (懷特先生,我有些建議。) B: Ok, come to my office and talk to me. (好的,到我辦公室裏來談談。) 
我已經徹底沒主意了。	**I´ve completely run out of ideas.** A: Alice, what about you? (愛麗絲,你覺得呢?) B: I've completely run out of ideas. (我已經徹底沒主意了。) 注解 run out of 意爲用完、耗盡。
我不喜歡把所有的事情都擱置不理。	**I hate to put everything on hold.**
也許我們在時間管理方面確實存在着一些問題。	**Maybe we do have some problems with time management.**
很高興您能及時抵達。	**I am glad you make it on time.**
一路順利吧?	**How was your flight?** A: How was your flight? (一路順利吧?) B: It was pretty bumpy. (路上顛簸得厲害。)
我很樂意陪您在城裏轉轉。	**I´d be happy to take you around the city.** 注解 I've already done something. 意爲:我已經做了某事。
您覺得這樣的安排可以嗎?	**How does that schedule sound to you?**

您一定累壞了。	**You must be tired.** A: You must be tired. (您一定累壞了。) B: Yes, a little bit. (是的，有點兒。) 注解 must be 是固定短語，意爲：一定是。後面可加形容詞，hungry (餓了)，happy (開心)等等。
我來幫你拿包吧。	**Let me help you with your bag.** A: Let me help you with your bag. (我來幫你拿包吧。) B: Thank you, you are so kind. (謝謝，你人真好。)
您是第一次來西雅圖嗎？	**Is it your first time to Seattle?** 注解 first time to... 意爲第一次……，後面可加地點，表示第一次到某個地方，也可在後面加 to do something，表示第一次做某事。
我已經爲您訂了旅館。	**I've already made a hotel reservation for you.**
我們先到旅館把東西放下。	**Let's go to the hotel first and drop off your things.** A: Let's go to the hotel first and drop off your things. (我們先到旅館把東西放下。) B: Great! That's just what I am thinking. (太好了，這正是我想的。) 
您在這期間想去哪裏看看？	**What would you like to see while you are here?**
我敢保證可以安排。	**I'm pretty sure it can be arranged.**
我可以當您的翻譯和導游。	**I can be your translator and tour guide.**
如果你沒意見，我們想請你吃飯。	**If you don't mind, we'd like to invite you to dinner.**
您如果有什麼疑問和問題，我會幫您解決。	**If you have any questions or problems, I will be right here to help you out.**

我想和您討論一下日程安排的問題。	I would like to discuss the schedule with you.
這是我們爲您擬定的活動日程安排。請過目一下,好嗎?	Here is a copy of the itinerary we have worked out for you. Would you please take a look at it?
我認爲現在可以先草擬一具臨時方案。	I think we can draw up a tentative plan now.
如果對某些細節有意見的話,請提出來。	If you have any questions on the details, feel free to ask.
歡迎到我們的工廠來。	Welcome to our factory.
今天由我來帶你們參觀。	I´ll be showing you around today.
參觀後您會對我們的產品有更深的了解。	You´ll know our products better after this visit.
也許我們可以先參觀一下設計部門。	Maybe we could start with the Designing Department.
然後我們再去看看生產綫。	Then we could look at the production line.
現在我們去下一個車間看看。	Here, let´s move to the next room.
墻上的圖表是工藝流程表。	These drawings on the wall are process sheets.
我們實行的工作是兩班倒。	We are running on two shifts.
幾乎每一道工藝都是由電腦控制的。	Almost every process is computerized.

Phone Calls
【電　　話】

- 打電話
- 接電話
- 電話留言
- 打錯電話

打電話 Make Telephone Calls

喂,我是琳達。	**Hello, this is Linda.** 注解 在打電話的時候，要說明自己的身份是用 this is...,而不是 I am...。
我是紐約黃金書店的李珊麗。	**This is Sunny Li from Golden Age Bookstore.**
喂,是喬治嗎?	**Hello, George?**
湯姆在嗎?	**Is Tom there?**
我想找威廉。	**May I speak to William?**
我要找你們老板。	**I´d like to speak to your boss.**
請問是大衛·格林醫生的辦公室嗎?	**Is that Dr. David Green´s office?** 注解 打電話時詢問對方也不是用"Are you...",應該用"Is that ..."。
真對不起，這麼晚了給您打電話。	**I must apologize for calling you so late.** 回 **I´m very sorry for calling you so late.** 注解 如果是太早給對方打電話可以把 late 替換爲 early。
我把你吵醒了嗎?	**Did I wake you up?**
請幫我轉客服。	**Please transfer me to the customer service department.**
請接分機 10。	**Extension 10, please.**
你剛打電話找我?	**Did you just call me?**
我給你回電話。	**I´m calling you back.**

接電話 Answer the Phone

我就是。	Speaking.
請問你是哪位?	Who´s calling, please? Who´s speaking, please?
時代出版社，您有什麼事?	Times Publishing, can I help you?
你好,請問你找誰?	Hello, who are you looking for?
你要找哪一位布朗小姐? 我們有兩位布朗小姐。	Which Miss Brown are you calling for? There are two Miss Brown.
請稍等。	Hold on, please. Wait a moment, please.
我讓她接電話。	I´ll put her on.
我幫你把電話轉給他。	I´ll transfer your call to him.
對不起，我現在不方便接電話。	Sorry, I can´t take the call right now.
抱歉，我聽不清楚你說的話。	Excuse me, I can´t hear you clearly.
我等一下回你電話。	I´ll call you back later.
他正在開會。	He´s in a meeting right now.
他出差了。	He´s on a business trip.

電話留言 Leaving a Message

你要他回電話嗎?	**Would you like to have him call you back?** A: Would you like to have him call you back? (你要他回電話嗎？) B: No, thank you. I'll call again later. (不用了，謝謝。我遲點再打。)
有什麼要我轉達的嗎?	**Is there anything I can pass on for you?** A: Is there anything I can pass on for you? (有什麼要我轉達的嗎？) B: Please tell him that Daisy called. (請告訴他黛絲給他打過電話。) 
你要留言嗎?	**Would you like to leave a message?**
波頓先生知道你的號碼嗎?	**Does Mr. Bolton have your phone number?**
你方便留下聯系方式嗎?	**Would you like to leave a contact number?** A: Would you like to leave a contact number? (你方便留下聯系方式嗎？) B: My number is 917-987-6543. (我的號碼是 917-987-6543。)
請告訴我你的電話號碼。	**Please tell me your phone number.** A: Please tell me your phone number. (請告訴我你的號碼。) B: You can reach me at 212-345-6789 until eight o'clock. (在 8 點之前可以打 212-345-6789 聯系我。)
請比利盡快回電話給我。	**Please ask Billy to call me back as soon as possible.**
他多晚回我電話都沒關系。	**It doesn´t matter how late he calls me back.**

打錯電話 Dialing a Wrong Number

你打錯電話了。

You got the wrong number.

A: Hello, is Susan there? (喂，蘇珊嗎？)

B: You got the wrong number. (你打錯電話了。)

沒有這個人。

There is nobody here by that name.

A: There is nobody here by that name.
(沒有這個人。)

B: May I check the phone number with you?
(可以跟你確認一下電話號碼嗎？)

我不是你要找的人。

I´m not the person you are calling for.

我們這是住宅。

This is a residential number.

A: Is that Golden Age Bookstore?
(請問是黃金書店嗎？)

B: No, this is a residential number.
(不是，我們這是住宅。)

她已經離職了。

She has left the job.

A: Hello, may I speak to Lisa? (請問麗莎在嗎？)

B: She has left the job. (她已經離職了。)

他已經不住這裏了。

He doesn´t live here anymore.

A: He doesn't live here anymore.
(他已經不住這裏了。)

B: Do you know his new address?
(你知道他的新地址嗎？)

你打的電話號碼是多少？

What number are you calling?

A: What number are you calling?
(你打的電話號碼是多少？)

B: 646-688-5622, are you using this number now?
(646-688-5622，這個號碼現在你用嗎？)

Entertainments
【娛　　樂】

- 購　物
  - 超　市
  - 便利店
  - 商　場
- 運　動
- 健身房
- 看電影
- 唱　K
- 音樂會
- 酒　吧
- 公　園

購 物 Shopping

超 市 Supermarket

家電區在哪裏?	**Where is the Home Appliance Section?** A: Where is the Home Appliance Section? (家電區在哪裏?) B: In the second aisle on this floor. (在這層樓的第二個過道。)
雨傘在哪兒?	**Where can I find an umbrella?** A: Where can I find an umbrella? (雨傘在哪兒?) B: In the second floor. (在二樓。)
有賣罐頭食品嗎?	**Do you have canned food?** A: Do you have canned food? (有賣罐頭食品嗎?) B: Yes, it's over there. (有,在那邊。)
有進口食品區嗎?	**Is there an International Foods Aisle?** A: Is there an International Foods Aisle? (有進口食品區嗎?) B: Sorry, we haven't. (抱歉,沒有。)
我想買意大利面。	**I´d like to buy some spaghetti.** A: Can I help you? (需要幫忙嗎?) B: I'd like to buy some spaghetti. (我想買意大利面。)
可以拿一個給我嗎?	**Could you take me one?** A: Could you take me one? (可以拿一個給我嗎?) B: Certainly. (當然。)
我拿不着。	**It´s out of my reach.** A: It's out of my reach. (我拿不着。) B: Let me help you. (讓我來幫你。)

賣完了。	**It´s sold out.**
那些蘋果很便宜。	**Those apples are cheap.** A: Those apples are cheap. (那些蘋果很便宜。) B: But they are not fresh. (但不新鮮。)
看起來很好吃。	**They look delicious.** A: How about those pears? (那些梨怎麼樣?) B: They look delicious. (看起來很好吃。)
什麼時候有新貨?	**When will you have new ones?** A: When will you have new ones? (什麼時候有新貨?) B: I'm not sure. (我不確定。)
這個今天打折嗎?	**Is this on sale today?**
促銷什麼時候結束?	**When is the sale over?** A: When is the sale over? (促銷什麼時候結束?) B: It's on sale until tomorrow. (到明天結束。)
促銷結束了。	**The sale is over.**
如果不打折就太貴了。	**It´s too expensive if it´s not on sale.**
你想要什麼牌子的?	**Which brand do you want?** A: Which brand do you want? (你想要什麼牌子的?) B: Any suggestions? (你有什麼建議嗎?)
哪個牌子比較受歡迎?	**Which brand is more popular?**
我要用現金付款。	**I will pay cash.**
付現金給打折扣嗎?	**Do you give discounts for cash?**

便利店 Convenience Store

你常去便利店嗎?

Do you often go to the convenience store?

A: Do you often go to the convenience store?
(你常去便利店嗎？)

B: Yeah, I go to the convenience store to buy a newspaper every day. (嗯，我每天去便利店買報紙。)

我去便利店繳費。

I go to pay my bills in the convenience store.

A: What do you do in the convenience store? (你去便利店做什麼？)

B: I go to pay my bills in the convenience store. (我去便利店繳費。)

注解 water bill 水費 electricity bill 電費；cell phone bill 手機費；credit card bill 信用卡費。

我經常用便利店的提款機。

I usually use the ATM machine in the convenience store.

A: Have you ever used the ATM machine in the convenience store? (你用過便利店的提款機嗎？)

B: I usually use the ATM machine in the convenience store. (我經常用便利店的提款機。)

你吃過便利店的便當嗎?

Have you ever eaten a lunchbox sold in the convenience store?

A: Have you ever eaten a lunchbox sold in the convenience store? (你吃過便利店的便當嗎？)

B: Yes, I sometimes go to the convenience store to buy lunch. (吃過，有時候我在便利店買午餐。)

我住的地方離便利店很遠。

The place I live is far from the convenience store.

你喜歡逛便利店嗎?

Do you like shopping in the convenience store?

A: Do you like shopping in the convenience store?
(你喜歡逛便利店嗎？)

B: I think shopping in the convenience store is fun for me.
(我覺得逛便利店是種樂趣。)

商 場 Department Store

商店幾點開門?	**When does the store open?** A: When does the store open? (商店幾點開門?) B: It opens at ten. (10 點。) 注解 open 替換爲 close,表示幾點關門。
衹是看看。	**Just looking.** A: What are you looking for? (你在找什麼呢?) B: Just looking. (衹是看看。)
我想買滋潤型的乳液。	**I´d like a moisturizing cream.** A: What kind of cream would you like? (你想要什麼類型的乳液?) B: I'd like a moisturizing cream. (我想買滋潤型的乳液。)
我衹要純天然的產品。	**I just want a product of natural ingredients.** A: How about this one? (這個可以嗎?) B: No. I just want a product of natural ingredients. (不。我衹要純天然的產品。)
我想要防曬粉餅。	**I want a UV protection powder cake.** A: I want a UV protection powder cake. (我想要防曬粉餅。) B: Ok. Let me show you. (好的,我拿給你看看。)
我喜歡味道清爽的香水。	**I like the perfume with fresh scent.** A: I like the perfume with fresh scent. (我喜歡味道清爽的香水。) B: Please have a look at this. (請您看看這個。) 
我需要遮瑕效果好點的粉餅。	**I need a facial powder with better cover effect.** A: What kind of powder cake do you want? (你想要哪種粉餅?) B: I need a facial powder with better cover effect. (我需要遮瑕效果好點的粉餅。)
防曬系數要 20。	**The UV protection level should be twenty.**

我不要膏狀的護膚品。	**I don´t need lotion-based care products.** A: Please look at this. (請看看這個。) B: I don't need lotion-based care products. (我不要膏狀的護膚品。)
有没有不含油脂的化妝品?	**Is there any oil free cosmetics?** A: Is there any oil free cosmetics? (有没有不含油脂的化妝品?) B: Sorry, we have none. (不好意思,没有。)
你們賣的口紅有哪些顏色?	**What shades of lipstick do you sell?** A: What shades of lipstick do you sell? (你們賣的口紅有哪些顏色?) B: Please look here. (請看這裏。)
我想要吸汗的材質。	**I want the sweat-absorbing material.**
我要 34 寸 B 罩杯。	**I want a thirty-four B bra.** A: Can you tell me your size? (可以告訴我你的尺寸嗎?) B: I want a thirty-four B bra. (我要 34 寸 B 罩杯。)
可以給我看看這條裙子嗎?	**Could you show me the skirt?** A: Could you show me the skirt? (可以給我看看這條裙子嗎?) B: Of course. (當然。)
這件 T 恤衫有藍色的嗎?	**Do you have this T-shirt in blue?** A: Do you have this T-shirt in blue? (這件 T 恤衫有藍色的嗎?) B: Please wait for a moment. Let me check. (請稍等 我去查查。) 
我喜歡三寸以上的高跟鞋。	**I like high-heels to be more than three inches.** A: Would you like flat-heeled or high-heeled shoes? (你要平底鞋還是高跟鞋?) B: I like high-heels to be more than three inches. (我喜歡三寸以上的高跟鞋。)

我喜歡圓頭的鞋子。	**I like round-tipped shoes.** A: What kind of shoes style are you looking for? (你要找什麼款式的鞋子？) B: I like round-tipped shoes. (我喜歡圓頭的鞋子。)
我要接近膚色的絲襪。	**I need a pair of nude color silk stockings.**
試衣間在哪裏?	**Where´s the fitting room?**
我可以試穿嗎?	**May I try it on?** A: May I try it on? (我可以試穿嗎？) B: Sorry, the products on sale cannot be tried on. (不好意思,特價商品不能試。)
太緊了。	**It´s too tight.** A: It's too tight. (太緊了。) B: You may try this one. (或許你可以試試這件。)
有大一號的嗎?	**Do you have one in a bigger size?** A: Do you have one in a bigger size? (有大一號的嗎？) B: Yes. I'll take it to you. (有,我去拿給你。) 
這個顏色不適合我的膚色。	**The color doesn´t fit my skin tone.** A: The color doesn't fit my skin tone. (這個顏色不適合我的膚色。) B: We have other colors for you to choose from. (還有別的顏色可以選。)
我覺得穿起來怪怪的。	**I feel odd wearing it.** A: I feel odd wearing it. (我覺得穿起來怪怪的。) B: I don't think so. You look good in it. (我不覺得。挺好看的。)
穿起來不舒服。	**I feel uncomfortable.**
裙子太短了。	**The skirt is too short.**

太露了。	**It exposes too much.**
你覺得這個適合我嗎?	**Do you think it matches me?** A: Do you think it matches me? (你覺得這個合適我嗎？) B: It suits you. (這個很適合你。)
質量不錯。	**The material is truly good.** A: The material is truly good. (質量不錯。) B: The material washes well. (這個料子很耐洗。)
太艷了。	**It´s too flashy.** A: It's too flashy. (太艷了。) B: But you fit the color. (但你很適合這個顏色。) 注解 flashy 可以替換爲 plain(素), loud(花哨)。
拉鏈不好拉。	**The zipper doesn´t zip well.** A: The zipper doesn't zip well. (拉鏈不好拉。) B: Don't worry. We have another one. (別擔心。我們有另外一件。)
褲子太長了。	**The pants are too long.** A: The pants are too long. (褲子太長了。) B: We can make the pants shorter. (我們可以把褲子改短一點。)
袖子太短了。	**The sleeves are too short.** A: The sleeves are too short. (袖子太短了。) B: What a pity. We just have this one left. (可惜了。我們衹有這一件了。)
大小剛剛好。	**It fits me well.** A: Does it fit you? (合適嗎？) B: It fits me well. (大小剛剛好。)
扣子扣不起來。	**I can´t button it up.** A: I can't button it up. (扣子扣不起來。) B: Please try the one a size up. (那試試大一號的吧。)

你可以幫我修改嗎?	**Do you think you can tailor it for me?** A: Do you think you can tailor it for me? (你可以幫我修改嗎?) B: Ok, no problem. (可以,沒問題。)
我喜歡穿寬鬆的衣服。	**I like to wear loose clothes.** A: I like to wear loose clothes. (我喜歡穿寬鬆的衣服。) B: This skin-tight design is popular this year. (今年比較流行貼身的設計。)
兩個我都想要。	**I want both of them.** A: I want both of them. (兩個我都想要。) B: These two are great. (這兩個都不錯的。)
我要這個。	**I´ll take this one.** A: I'll take this one. (我要這個。) B: Ok. Let me wrap it for you. (好的,我幫你包起來。)

能再便宜一些嗎?	**Would you give me a discount?** A: Would you give me a discount? (能再便宜一些嗎?) B: How about I give you a 5 dollar discount? (少 5 美元怎樣?)
太貴了。	**That´s too expensive.** A: That's too expensive. (太貴了。) B: How about 80 dollars? (80 美元怎麼樣?)
我祇有這些錢了。	**I only have this much money.** A: I only have this much money. (我祇有這些錢了。) B: I only make six dollars of profit for each piece. (我一件祇賺 6 美元。)
算整數吧?	**How about making it an even price?** A: How about making it an even price? (算整數吧?) B: It's already cheap. (已經很便宜了。)
請給我包一下。	**Please wrap it.**

別人衹賣 200 美元。	**Others sell it for two hundred dollars.** A: Others sell it for two hundred dollars. (別人衹賣 200 美元。) B: Impossible. (不可能。)
這件衣服有瑕疵，便宜點給我。	**This piece of clothing has some flaws, I´ll buy it under a discount.** A: This piece of clothing has some flaws, I'll buy it under a discount. (這件衣服有瑕疵,便宜點給我。) B: The price for you takes the flaw into account. (就是有瑕疵才給你這個價格的。)
要不你送個禮物給我?	**Can you give me a small gift?** A: Can you give me a small gift? (要不你送個禮物給我?) B: You are so good at bargaining. (你真會講價。)
我是老客户了，別跟我計較了。	**I´m your old customer. Don´t be too critical on this.** A: I'm your old customer. Don't be too critical on this. (我是老客户了,別跟我計較了。) B: I can't go any cheaper than that. (不能再便宜了。)
衹有這個顏色了，算便宜點。	**This is the only color you have left.** **I´ll take it under a cheaper price.**  A: This is the only color you have left. I'll take it under a cheaper price. (衹有這個顏色了,算便宜點。) B: I'm selling it at less cost. (我已經賠本了。)
應該再便宜點。	**The price should be cheaper.** A: The price should be cheaper. (應該再便宜點。) B: One hundred dollars. Take it or leave it. (100 美元,買不買隨便你。)
修改可不可以不要另外收費啊?	**Can you tailor it without extra charge?** A: Can you tailor it without extra charge? (修改可不可以不要另外收費啊?) B: It costs only this much money. (不差這一點錢啦!)

便宜點，我會介紹朋友過來的買的。	**Give me a cheaper price, or I won´t bring my friends here.** A: Give me a cheaper price, or I won't bring my friends here. (便宜點，我會介紹朋友過來買的。) B: Remember to bring your friends here. (記得帶朋友過來買哦！)
請幫我用禮盒包起來。	**Please pack it in a gift box.**
我要塑料袋。	**I need a plastic bag.**
包裝要另外付費嗎?	**Does packing cost extra charge?**
請幫我把價錢標簽撕掉。	**Please tear off the price tag.**
請幫我包裝一下。	**Please help me pack it.** A: Please help me pack it. (請幫我包裝一下。) B: Ok. Please wait for a moment. (好的，請稍等。) 
是自己用的，不用包了。	**This is for my own use. I don´t need to pack it.**
包裝得真漂亮，謝謝。	**You pack it so pretty. Thank you.**
麻煩你了。	**Thank you for the service.**
我要放一張卡片進去。	**I want to put a card inside.**
祇能用現金嗎?	**Do you only take cash?**
我可以分期付款嗎?	**Can I pay by installment payment?**
我可以用支票嗎?	**Can I write a check?**
可以用信用卡支付嗎?	**Do you accept credit cards?**

這個多少錢?	How much is it?
這些總共多少錢?	How much are these in total?
這個不是打六折嗎?	Isn´t this at a forty percent discount?
不是有贈品嗎?	Isn´t there a gift?
貴賓卡可以打幾折?	How much of a discount can I get through my VIP card?
可以換貨嗎?	Can I exchange it?
可以退款嗎?	Can I have a refund?
我要退貨。	I´d like to return it.
我要換小一號的。	I want to exchange it for a smaller size. 注解 smaller 可以替換爲 bigger,表示大一號的。
我要換長一點的。	I want to exchange it for a longer one. 注解 longer 可以替換爲 shorter,表示短一點的。
我要換粉紅色的。	I want to exchange it for pink.
這件衣服還沒穿就破了,我要退錢。	This piece of clothing was torn before I wore it. I want a refund.
爲什麼我不能退貨?	Why can´t I return this item? A: Why can't I return this item? (爲什麼我不能退貨?) B: If the cosmetics has no quality problem, no refund allowed. (化妝品無質量問題概不退換。)
其它產品我都不喜歡,我要退錢。	I don´t like any of your other products. I want a refund.
我要換另外一件。	I want to exchange it for another one.

運 動 Exercise

我在户外做運動。	**I do exercise outdoor.** A: Where do you do excercise? (你在什麼地方運動？) B: I do exercise outdoor. (我在户外做運動。)
我傍晚做運動。	**I do exercise at evening.** A: When do you exercise? (你什麼時候運動？) B: I do exercise at evening. (我傍晚做運動。)
我討厭做運動。	**I don´t like doing exercise.** A: I think you lack exercise. (我想你缺乏運動。) B: I don't like doing exercise. (我討厭做運動。)
我每天運動半小時。	**I exercise for half an hour every day.** A: How long do you exercise for every day? (你每天運動多久？) B: I exercise for half an hour every day. (我每天運動半小時。)
你平常做什麼運動?	**What do you usually do for exercise?** A: What do you usually do for exercise? (你平常做什麼運動？) B: I seldom take exercise. (我很少運動。)
你喜歡跑步嗎?	**Do you like running?** A: Do you like running? (你喜歡跑步嗎？) B: No. I hate running most. (不喜歡，我最討厭的就是跑步。)
我運動爲了减肥。	**I take exercise for losing weight.** A: I take exercise for losing weight. (我運動爲了减肥。) B: But you look thin. (但你看起來不胖。)

我把家務當作運動。	**I consider housework as exercise.** A: I consider housework as exercise. (我把家務當作運動。) B: You can kill two birds with one stone. (你真是一舉兩得。)
我沒有時間做運動。	**I have no time doing sports.**
游泳是我最喜歡的運動。	**Swimming is my favorite sport.** A: Swimming is my favorite sport. (游泳是我最喜歡的運動。) B: When did you learn swimming? (你什麼時候學游泳的？)
爬樓梯也是不錯的運動。	**Climbing stairs is also a good exercise.** A: Climbing stairs is also a good exercise. (爬樓梯是不錯的運動。) B: I climb stairs to office every day. (我每天爬樓梯上辦公室。)
近幾年,瑜伽很受歡迎。	**In recent years, yoga is very popular.** A: In recent years, yoga is very popular. (近幾年,瑜伽很受歡迎。) B: I try to play it recently. (我最近也在練。) 
運動有益身體健康。	**Exercise is good for our health.**
我習慣在晚飯後散步。	**I´m used to go for a walk after supper.**
你會打棒球嗎？	**Can you play baseball?** A: Can you play baseball? (你會打棒球嗎？) B: No. I just can play tennis. (不會。我衹會打網球。)
你喜歡哪類運動？	**What kind of sports do you like?**
如果我步行上班，即可以鍛煉身體又可以省錢。	**If I walk to work, I can get some exercise as well as saving money.**

健身房 Gym

我想加入你們的健身俱樂部。	**I´d like to join your gym.** A: I'd like to join your gym. (我想加入你們的健身俱樂部。) B: Would you like to be a member or a vip? (你想成爲普通會員還是貴賓會員？)
你們有哪些服務?	**What service do you offer?**
成爲會員要交多少錢?	**How much does a membership cost?**
我一個星期健身兩次。	**I work out twice a week.** A: How many times do you work out a week? (你一個星期健身幾次？) B: I work out twice a week. (我一個星期健身兩次。)
練瑜伽能減肥嗎?	**Can I lose weight by doing yoga?** A: Can I lose weight by doing yoga? (練瑜伽能減肥嗎？) B: It depends on the time and force you practice. (這要看你的練習時間以及運動量。)
我每天去健身房跳健身操。	**I go to gym to do setting -up exercises every day.** A: Are you interested in gym? (你對健身房有興趣嗎？) B: Yeah. I go to gym to do setting-up exercises every day. (有啊。我每天去健身房跳健身操。) 
我想這會有所幫助的。	**I think it will be helpful.** A: Does it work? (練習這個有用嗎？) B: I think it will be helpful. (我想這會有所幫助的。)

你看起來精力充沛。	**You look energetic.**
這個健身機械有什麼功能?	**What´s the function of this body building equipment?** A: What's the function of this body building equipment? (這個健身機械有什麼功能?) B: It can help you strengthen the arm muscle. (可以鍛煉手臂肌肉。)
怎麼用呢?	**How to use it?**
我想腰瘦一點，有什麼建議嗎?	**I want to make my waist thinner. Do you have any suggestions?**
我想瘦腿要怎麼做?	**What should I do if I want to make my legs thinner?**
我每周應該用幾次跑步機?	**How many times should I use the treadmill every week?** A: How many times should I use the treadmill every week? (我每周應該用幾次跑步機?) B: Three times is enough for you. (對你來說三次夠了。)
這個會不會很難?	**Is it difficult?**
我擔心我堅持不了。	**I´m afraid I can´t keep up.**
好像沒什麼用。	**It seems of little use.**
這個對我有幫助嗎?	**Is it helpful for me?**
你每次去健身多長時間?	**How long do you work out every time?** A: How long do you work out every time? (你每次去健身多長時間?) B: About one hour. (一個小時左右。)
健身可以保持身材。	**Workout helps keep in shape.**

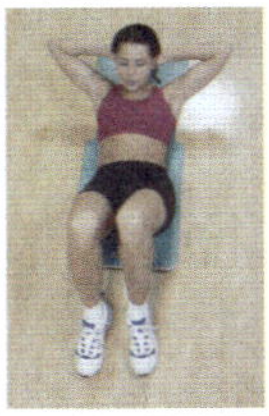

看電影 Seeing a Movie

去看電影嗎?	**How about going to a movie?** **回 Would you like to go to a movie?** A: How about going to a movie? (去看電影嗎?) B: Good idea. (好主意。)
我們去看電影吧。	**Let´s go to see a movie.** A: Let's go to see a movie. (我們去看電影吧。) B: Good. I want to see *Iron Man II*. (好啊! 我想看《鋼鐵俠 2》。)
今晚放什麼電影?	**What will be on tonight?** A: What will be on tonight? (今晚放什麼電影?) B: *Alice in Wonderland* and *Clash of the Titans*. (《愛麗絲夢游仙境》和《諸神之戰》。)
買票了嗎?	**Have you got the tickets?** A: Have you got the tickets? (買票了嗎?) B: No, the tickets are sold out. (没買到,賣完了。)
還有晚上 10 點的票嗎?	**Is there any tickets for ten o´clock left?** A: Is there any tickets for ten o'clock left? (還有晚上 10 點的票嗎?) B: Yes. How many tickets do you want? (還有。你要幾張?)
你覺得這部電影怎樣?	**What do you think of this movie?** A: What do you think of this movie? (你覺得這部電影怎麼樣?) B: Wonderful! (很精彩!)
太無聊了,看得我都睡着了。	**It´s so boring that I fall asleep.**

這部電影演多長時間?	**How long does the movie last?** **How long does the movie play?** A: How long does the movie last? (這部電影演多長時間?) B: One hundred and twenty-four minutes. (124 分鐘。)
這電影是誰演的?	**Who´s in the movie?** A: Who's in the movie? (這部電影是誰演的？) B: Anne Li. (李安妮。)
太長了。	**It´s too long.** A: It's too long. (太長了。) B: I think so too. (我也覺得。)
很有意思。	**That´s interesting.** A: That's interesting. (很有意思。) B: The plot is funny. (劇情很好玩。)
很讓人感動。	**It touches me.** A: It touches me. (很讓人感動。) B: Have you cried? (你哭了嗎？)
這個電影太悶了。	**The movie is too dull.** A: The movie is too dull. (這個電影太悶了。) B: It has a simple plot. (劇情太簡單了。)
我根本理解不了這部電影。	**I can´t understand this movie.** A: I can't understand this movie. (我根本理解不了這部電影。) B: Let me explain it for you. (我解釋給你聽吧。)
挺有意義的。	**It´s meaningful.** A: It's meaningful. (挺有意義的。) B: I like it very much. (我很喜歡。)
情節有點復雜。	**The plot is a little complex.** 注解 complex 可以替換爲 simple 簡單的。
成龍表演不錯。	**Jackie Chan did a great job.**

你最喜歡的影星是誰?	**Who is your favorite movie star?** A: Who is your favorite movie star? (你最喜歡的影星是誰?) B: Johnny Depp. I like his *Pirates of Caribbean*. (約翰尼·戴普。我很喜歡他的《加勒比海盜》。)
你知道戛納電影節嗎?	**Do you know the Cannes International Film Festival?** A: Do you know the Cannes International Film Festival? (你知道戛納電影節嗎?) B: Of course I know. It's so famous. (當然知道,這麼有名。) 注解 國際五大電影節:戛納電影節 Cannes International Film Festival,柏林電影節 Berlin Film Festival,威尼斯電影節 Venice Film Festival,蒙特利爾世界電影節 World Film Festival in Montreal,卡羅維發利電影節 Karlovy Vary Film Festival。
這部電影獲得奧斯卡最佳影片。	**This movie won the best picture of Oscar.** 注解 best director 最佳導演,best actress 最佳女主角,best actor 最佳男主角,best supporting actress 最佳女配角,best supporting actor 最佳男配角,best music 最佳音樂,best original screenplay 最佳原創劇本,best art direction 最佳藝術指導。
你喜歡看什麼電影?	**What film do you like to see?** A: What film do you like to see? (你喜歡看什麼電影?) B: Tragedy. (悲劇。) 注解 comedy 喜劇。
你喜歡看哪類電影?	**What kind of movies do you prefer?** A: What kind of movies do you prefer? (你喜歡看哪類電影?) B: I like science fictions. (我喜歡看科幻片。) 注解 musicals 音樂片,dracula movie 恐怖片,swordsmen film 武俠片,action movie 動作片,detective film 偵探片,ethical film 倫理片,affectional film 愛情片。
這是《暮光之城》的續集。	**This is the sequel of *Twilight*.**

唱 K KTV

一起去唱歌嗎?	**Should we go to karaoke?** A: Should we go to karaoke? (一起去唱歌嗎？) B: Ok. I like singing very much. (好啊。我最喜歡唱歌了。)
我五音不全。	**I´m tone-deaf.** 回 **I can´t carry a tune.** A: How about a song? (唱一首吧！) B: No. I'm tone-deaf. (不行，我五音不全。)
我們先點歌吧。	**Let´s order songs first.**
你唱得真好!	**You sing so well!** 回 **You´re a good singer.** A: You sing so well! (你唱得真好！) B: Thank you. (謝謝！)
到你了。	**It´s your turn now.** A: It's your turn now. (到你了。) B: I'm shy about singing in public. (我不好意思在很多人面前唱歌。)
你想唱什麼歌?	**What do you want to sing?** A: What do you want to sing? (你想唱什麼歌？) B: Let me see. (讓我想想。)
你哪首歌唱得最好?	**Which song do you sing best?** A: Which song do you sing best? (你哪首歌唱得最好？) B: Fly to your heart. (飛向你的心。)
我們好好玩吧。	**Let´s enjoy ourselves.** A: Let's sing troubles away. (讓我們把煩惱唱走。) B: Let's enjoy ourselves. (我們好好玩吧。)

音樂會 Concert

你經常聽音樂嗎?	**Do you listen to music often?** A: Do you listen to music often? (你經常聽音樂嗎？) B: I listen to music every day. (我天天都要聽音樂。)
你喜歡哪種音樂?	**What kind of music do you like?** A: What kind of music do you like? (你喜歡哪種音樂？) B: Jazz and pop music. (爵士和流行音樂。) 注解 rock and roll 搖滾樂，R&B 節奏布魯斯，rap 說唱音樂，light music 輕音樂，classical music 古典樂，symphony 交響樂。
我有很多 CD。	**I have a lot of CDs.** A: I have a lot of CDs. (我有很多 CD。) B: Wow! May I have a look? (哇！可以看一下嗎？)
你會什麼樂器?	**What instrument can you play?**  A: What instrument can you play? (你會什麼樂器？) B: I can play guitar. (我會彈吉他。) 注解 bass 貝斯，cello 大提琴，flute 長笛，jazz tomtom 爵士鼓，piano 鋼琴，saxophone 薩克斯，violin 小提琴。
我要訂兩張 6 月 15 日的票。	**I´d like to book two tickets for June.15.** A: I'd like to book two tickets for June.15. (我要訂兩張 6 月 15 日的票。) B: Ok. May I have your name? (好的。請問您怎麼稱呼？)
音樂會的票可以預定了。	**Tickets for the concert are on sale.** A: Tickets for the concert are on sale. (音樂會的票可以預定了。) B: Really? By telephone or on Internet? (真的嗎？是電話訂票還是網上訂票？)

下周三晚上有一場音樂會。	**There will be a concert next Wednesday.** A: There will be a concert next Wednesday. (下周三晚上有一場音樂會。) B: Are you going? (你打算去聽嗎？)
還有什麼時候的票?	**What date do you have tickets for?** A: What date do you have tickets for? (還有什麼時候的票？) B: Sorry, there're only tickets for next month left. (抱歉，衹有下個月的票了。)
我什麼時候要確認訂票?	**When should I confirm this booking?** A: When should I confirm this booking? (我什麼時候要確認訂票？) B: Twenty-four hours before the concert. (音樂會前 24 小時。)
音樂會幾點開始?	**When does the concert start?** A: When does the concert start? (音樂會幾點開始？) B: Eight o'clock. (八點。)
音樂會在哪裏舉行?	**Where will the concert held?** A: Where will the concert held? (音樂會在哪裏舉行？) B: In the music hall. (在音樂廳。)
什麼音樂會?	**What concert is it?**  A: I'm going to a concert tonight. (我今晚要去聽音樂會。) B: What concert is it? (什麼音樂會？)
哪個樂團的表演?	**Which band perform?** A: Which band perform? (哪個樂團的表演？) B: A band from Scotland. (一個蘇格蘭的樂團。)
音樂會幾點結束?	**When will the concert end?** A: When will the concert end? (音樂會幾點結束？) B: At ten thirty. (十點半。)
太震撼了!	**It´s convulsing!**

他們是我最喜歡的樂隊。	**They are my favorite band.** A: They are my favorite band. (他們是我最喜歡的樂隊。) B: It's a very successful band. (這是一支很成功的樂隊。)
我是他們的粉絲。	**I´m their fans.** A: Do you like them? (你喜歡他們嗎？) B: Of course. I'm their fans. (當然。我是他們的粉絲。)
他們的表演太棒了。	**Their performance were so awesome!** A: Their performance were so awesome. (他們的表演太棒了。) B: I was attracted by their performance completely. (我完全被他們的表演吸引了。)
這場音樂會太精彩了。	**The concert is very excellent.**
他們表演了最好的作品。	**They performed their best songs.** A: They performed their best songs. (他們表演了最好的作品。) B: Wow! You were so happy, weren't you? (哇！那你不是很開心？)
這跟聽 CD 是很不同的。	**It´s very different from listening to CDs.** A: It's very different from listening to CDs. (這跟聽 CD 是很不同的。) B: The prices are very different, too. (價格也很不同啊！)
這音樂真好聽！	**What beautiful music!**
他的表演很完美。	**His performance is perfect.**
歌手唱得很投入。	**The singer sings very devotedly.**
我喜歡那個鼓手。	**I like the drummer.** A: I like the drummer. (我喜歡那個鼓手。) B: Why? (爲什麼？)

這是我聽過最好聽的音樂會。	**This is the best concert I have ever been to.** A: What do you think of the concert? (音樂會怎麼樣？) B: This is the best concert I have ever been to. (這是我聽過最好聽的音樂會。)
這裏的燈光和音響都是一流的。	**The lighting and acoustics are first-class.** A: The lighting and acoustics are first-class. (這裏的燈光和音響都是一流的。) B: That's the reason why the ticket is so expensive. (這就是爲什麼它的票價這麼高了。)
票價很貴，但值得。	**The ticket is expensive, but it deserves.**
這個劇院很華麗。	**This theater is luxurious.**
在這裏聽音樂會很享受。	**It´s enjoyable to listen to music here.** A: It's enjoyable to listen to music here. (在這裏聽音樂會很享受。) B: It really is. (是啊。)
我喜歡這個音樂廳的氛圍。	**I like the atmosphere of the music hall.**
我喜歡聽現場的音樂。	**I like to listen to live music.**

我們的位子真不錯。	**We have great seats.** A: We have great seats. (我們的位子真不錯。) B: We can watch their performance clearly. (可以看清楚他們的表演。)
再來一次！	**Encore! Bravo, bravo!**
我對 10 年前的那場演唱會仍記憶猶新。	**I still have memories of that concert 10 years ago.** A: Do you remember that concert ten years ago? (還記得 10 年前的那場演唱會嗎？) B: I still have memories of that concert 10 years ago. (我對 10 年前的那場演唱會仍記憶猶新。)

酒 吧 Bar

在酒吧閑混。	**Hang out in a bar.** A: What are you doing? (你在做什麼？) B: Hang out in a bar. (在酒吧閑混。) 注解 hang out 在口語中通常是指閑逛的意思。
我們照例去酒吧。	**We make our ritual visit to the bar.** A: Where are you going after work? (下班後去哪裏？) B: We make our ritual visit to the bar. (我們照例去酒吧。)
我們去酒吧放鬆一下。	**Let´s have fun in a bar.** A: How boring the work is! (好無聊的工作！) B: Forget it. Let's have fun in a bar. (忘了吧，我們去酒吧放鬆一下。)
我要去酒吧喝酒。	**I´ll go to the bar for a drink.** A: I'll go to the bar for a drink. (我要去酒吧喝酒。) B: I'm going with. (我也一起去。)
你知道哪些酒吧好點嗎？	**Do you know any good bars?** A: Do you know any good bars? (你知道哪些酒吧好點嗎？) B: Sorry, I seldom go to the bar. (不好意思，我很少去酒吧。)
我非常喜歡。	**I like it very much.** A: How do you like this cocktail? (你喜歡這款雞尾酒嗎？) B: I like it very much. (我非常喜歡。) 
對我而言太烈了。	**It´s too strong for me.** A: How do you like vodka? (你喜歡伏特加嗎？) B: It's too strong for me. (對我而言太烈了。)

你要喝什麼?	**What would you like to drink?** A: What would you like to drink? (你要喝什麼?) B: Lemon juice. (檸檬汁。) 注解 在酒吧主要有兩大類飲料：含酒精的 liquor 和不含酒精的 soft drinks。常見的飲料：beer 啤酒，cherry 雪利酒，champagne 香檳酒，wine 葡萄酒，cocktail 雞尾酒，whisky 威士忌，brandy 白蘭地，bubbling wine 汽酒，fruit juice 水果果汁——orange juice 橙汁，lemon juice 檸檬汁，tomato juice 西紅柿汁，etc.，cola 可樂，mineral water 礦泉水。
你要喝什麼酒?	**What liquor do you prefer?**
老實説，我不喜歡這種酒。	**Frankly speaking, I don´t like this wine.** A: Shall I pour you out a glass of Wisky? (我給您倒杯威士忌好吗?) B: Frankly speaking, I don't like this wine. (老实说，我不喜欢这种酒。) 
我要一杯杜鬆子酒。	**I´d like a gin.** A: What wine would you like? (你喝什麼酒?) B: I'd like a gin. (我要一杯杜鬆子酒。)
我建議您試一下這款啤酒。	**I suggest you have a taste of this beer.** A: I suggest you have a taste of this beer. (我建議您試一下這款啤酒。) B: That's a good idea. (這是一個好主意。)
純的還是加冰塊的?	**Straight or on the rocks?** A: Bring us a bottle of Scotch whisky. (給我們來一瓶蘇格蘭威士忌。) B: Straight or on the rocks? (純的還是加冰塊的?)
要純的。	**I prefer straight.**
要加冰的。	**I´d like it on the rocks.**
再給我另一杯。	**Make it two.** A: Make it two. (再給我另一杯。) B: Ok. Please wait for a moment. (好的，請稍等。)

你可以介紹點好酒嗎?	**Can you recommend some good wine?** A: Can you recommend some good wine? (你可以介紹點好酒嗎?) B: We have a wine that has been preserved for 15 years. (我們有一支保存了 15 年的紅酒。)
我還很清醒。	**I´m still sober.**
我喝醉了。	**I´m drunk.** A: I'm drunk. (我喝醉了。) B: Your tolerance level for alcohol degraded. (你酒量變小了。)
我們坐在酒吧裏談天説地。	**We sat around in the bar, shooting the breeze.** A: You stayed for a long time in the bar yesterday. (你們昨天在酒吧呆了好久啊!) B: We sat around in the bar, shooting the breeze. (我們坐在酒吧裏談天説地。) 注解 shooting the breeze 就是在很輕鬆、很愉快的氣氛下和朋友聊天。 
這個位子没人坐的嗎?	**Is this seat empty?** A: Is this seat empty? (這個位子没人坐的嗎?) B: Yes, and this one will be if you sit down. (是的,如果你坐下,我的位子就是空的。)
我想我能讓你非常快樂。	**I think I could make you very happy.** A: I think I could make you very happy. (我想我能讓你非常快樂。) B: Why? Are you leaving? (是嗎? 你是説你要走了嗎?)
這個酒吧不錯。	**This is a nice bar.** A: This is a nice bar. (這個酒吧不錯。) B: I don't want to leave. (不想離開了。)
服務員,請拿帳單來!	**Waiter, bill, Please!** A: Waiter, bill, Please! (服務員,請拿帳單來!) B: Would you care to have separate bills or one bill? (帳單開在一起還是分開?)

總共是多少錢?	**How much is the total charge?** A: Here is your bill, sir. (先生,這是您的賬單。) B: How much is the total charge? (總共是多少錢?)
今晚過得很開心。	**We have a good time tonight.**
一共多少錢?	**What will it be together?**
請收錢。	**There you are.** A: There you are. (請收錢。) B: Thank you very much, Sir. Do come again, Please! (謝謝,歡迎再來。)
通宵營業 。	**Open all night.** A: How late is it open? (營業到幾點?) B: Open all night. (通宵營業 。)
你昨晚跌跌撞撞地走出酒吧。	**You fumbled your way out of the bar last night.** A: You fumbled your way out of the bar last night. (你昨晚跌跌撞撞地走出酒吧。) B: Really? I couldn't recall. (是嗎? 我記不起來了。)
我喝了威士忌會感到頭暈目眩。	**The whisky will make my head swim.** A: Do you drink whisky? (你喝威士忌嗎?) B: The whisky will make my head swim. (我喝了威士忌會感到頭暈目眩。)
古典鷄尾酒的基酒是威士忌。	**The base of Old Fashioned cocktail is whiskey.** A: The base of Old Fashioned cocktail is whiskey. (古典鷄尾酒的基酒是威士忌。) B: That is so. (原來如此。)
法國紅酒非常受歡迎。	**Red wines from France are very popular.** A: What wine do you recommend? (你推薦什麼酒?) B: Red wines from France are very popular. Would you like one? (法國紅酒非常受歡迎。要來一杯嗎?)

公園 Park

我要去公園。	**I am going to the park.** A: Are you free this afternoon? (今天下午有空嗎？) B: I am going to the park. (我要去公園。)
公園越來越美了。	**The park is becoming more and more beautiful.** A: The park has changed a lot! (這個公園變化好大啊！) B: The park is becoming more and more beautiful. (公園越來越美了。)
黄石國家公園到了。	**Here we are – Yellowstone National Park.** A: Here we are - Yellowstone National Park. (黄石國家公園到了。) B: We're here. (我們到了。)
跟我一起去公園散步好嗎?	**How about having a brisk walk in the park with me?** A: How about having a brisk walk in the park with me? (跟我一起去公園散步好嗎？) B: Sorry, I have other plans. (不好意思，我有其他事情。)
我們騎自行車去公園。	**We go to the park by bike.** A: How do you go to the park? (你們怎樣去公園？) B: We go to the park by bike. (我們騎自行車去公園。)
昨天我去公園了。	**I went to the park yesterday.** A: I went to the park yesterday. (昨天我去公園了。) B: So did I. But I didn't see you. (我也去了。但沒看到你。)
我們在公園裏玩。	**We are playing in the park.** A: Aren't you at home? (你們都不在家嗎？) B: We are playing in the park. (我們在公園裏玩。)

公園裏有好多楓樹。	**There are many maples in the park.** A: There are many maples in the park. (公園裏有好多楓樹。) B: It must be very beautiful in fall. (到了秋天這裏一定很美。)
去中央公園怎麽樣?	**What about Central Park?** A: What about Central Park? (去中央公園怎麽樣?) B: It sounds good. (這主意不錯。)
你喜歡卡霍恩紀念公園嗎?	**Do you like Cahoon Memorial Park?** A: Do you like Cahoon Memorial Park? (你喜歡卡霍恩紀念公園嗎?) B: I haven't been there. (我没去過那兒。)
晚飯後，我們喜歡去公園聊天。	**After supper, we like to chat in the park.** A: After supper, we like to chat in the park. (晚飯後,我們喜歡去公園聊天。) B: You are so romantic! (你們好浪漫啊!)
你到公園去嗎?	**Will you go to the park?** A: Will you go to the park? (你到公園去嗎?) B: No, I need to go to the library. (不去,我要去圖書館。)
公園裏有個人工湖。	**There is a man–made lake in the park.** A: There is a man-made lake in the park. (公園裏有個人工湖。) B: Can you show me there? (能帶我去看看嗎?)
我們去公園野餐吧。	**Let´s go for a picnic in the park.** A: It's a fine day. Let's go for a picnic in the park. (今天天氣不錯!我們去公園野餐吧。) B: That's good! (好啊!) 
公園上午七點半開門。	**The park opens at 7:30 a.m..** A: The park opens at 7:30 a.m.. (公園上午七點半開門。) B: When shall we leave? (那我們什麽時候出發?)
公園裏人不會多。	**There won´t be too many people in the park.**

你想到公園走走嗎?	**Would you care for a walk in the park?** A: Would you care for a walk in the park? (你想到公園走走嗎？) B: Yes, I'd love to. (好啊。)
你到公園要多久?	**How long do you need to get to the park?** A: How long do you need to get to the park? (你到公園要多久？) B: It's about ten minutes' walk. (走路十分鐘就到。)
公園的入口在哪裏?	**Where is the entrance to the park?** A: Where is the entrance to the park? (公園的入口在哪裏？) B: We have to ask somebody. (得問一下人。)
我們在公園會合。	**We will meet in the park.** A: Shall I come to pick you up? (要我去接你嗎？) B: No. We will meet in the park. (不用。我們在公園會合。)
這個公園太引人入勝了。	**It is a fascinating park.**
我們中午到公園。	**We´ll arrive at the park at noon.** A: When will you arrive? (你們什麼時候能到？) B: We'll arrive at the park at noon. (我們中午到公園。)
這個公園野生動物很多。	**Wild animals abounds in this park.** A: Wild animals abounds in this park. (這個公園野生動物很多。) B: It's good. I love animals. (好啊。我喜歡動物。)
公園裏飄溢着花香。	**The park is brimming with the fragrance of flowers.**  A: The park is brimming with the fragrance of flowers. (公園裏飄溢着花香。) B: It's comfortable to stay here. (在這裏真舒服。)
公園裏鮮花盛開。	**Flowers are springing up in the park.**

這裏空氣清新!

The air is very fresh!

公園正中有一個噴泉。

There is a fountain at the centre of the park.

A: There is a fountain at the centre of the park. (公園正中有一個噴泉。)
B: Let's go to have a look. (我們去看看吧。)

假日我常去公園。

I often go to the park on holidays.

A: I often go to the park on holidays. (假日我常去公園。)
B: What are you doing there? (你在公園做什麼?)

我每天和女兒在公園裏玩。

I play with my daughter in the park every day.

A: I play with my daughter in the park every day. (我每天和女兒在公園裏玩。)
B: You're so happy. (真幸福。)

有時我去公園跑步。

Sometimes I jog in the park.

A: Sometimes I jog in the park. (有時我去公園跑步。)
B: You can ask me to jog with you next time. (下次可以叫上我一起跑。)

我每天都在公園遛狗。

I walk my dog in the park every day.

A: Where do you walk your dog? (你在哪裏遛狗?)
B: I walk my dog in the park every day. (我每天都在公園遛狗。)

心情不好的時候我喜歡一個人在公園坐一整天。

I like to sit in the park all day when I have a bad mood.

A: I like to sit in the park all day when I have a bad mood. (心情不好的時候我喜歡一個人在公園坐一整天。)
B: Interesting! (有意思!)

我還沒去過公園。

I haven´t been to the park.

A: I haven't been to the park. (我還沒去過公園。)
B: Impossible! (不可能!)

孩子們在公園做游戲。

Children are playing games in the park.

Travel
【旅　　行】

- 搭乘交通工具
- 訂　票
- 簽　證
- 體檢 & 檢疫
- 入　境
- 遺失行李
- 海關申報
- 機場旅游資訊
- 機位查詢、確認
- 機場用語
- 住　宿
- 用　餐
- 觀　光

搭乘交通工具 Transportation Tool

我坐飛機去澳大利亞。

I go to Australia by air.

A: How do you go to Australia?
(你怎樣去澳大利亞？)
B: I go to Australia by air. (我坐飛機去澳大利亞。)

我喜歡坐火車去。

I prefers to go by train.

A: Let's go by air. (我們坐飛機去吧。)
B: I disagree. I prefers to go by train.
(我不贊成，我喜歡坐火車去。)

我不能坐船，我會暈船的。

I can´t go by ship. I have seasickness.

A: Travelling by ship is the best choice.
(坐船去旅行是最佳的選擇。)
B: I can't go by ship. I have seasickness.
(我不能坐船，我會暈船的。)

下車吧，我們走路去。

Get off the bus. Let´s walk.

A: We are stuck in the traffic. (我們遇上塞車了。)
B: Get off the bus. Let's walk. (下車吧，我們走路去。)

這輛車是去機場的嗎?

Does this bus go to the airport?

A: Does this bus go to the airport?
(這輛車是去機場的嗎？)
B: I guess so. (我想是的。)

麻煩您到站時告訴我一聲。

Could you tell me when to get off?

A: Could you tell me when to get off?
(麻煩您到站時告訴我一聲。)
B: No problem. (沒問題。)

在哪兒能坐上快車?

Where can I catch an express train?

注解 a limited express 是特快車，而每站都停的車是 a local train 普通車或是慢，night train 則是夜車。

訂 票 Booking a Ticket

你訂票了嗎?	**Have you booked a ticket?** A: Have you booked a ticket? (你訂票了嗎?) B: Yes, I have booked the ticket three days in advance. (訂了,我提前三天訂的票。)
你想買單程票還是雙程票?	**Do you want a one-way ticket or a round-trip ticket?** A: Do you want a one-way ticket or a round-trip ticket? (你想買單程票還是雙程票?) B: Round-trip ticket, please. (雙程票,謝謝。)
雙程票一張多少錢?	**How much is a round-trip ticket?** A: How much is a round-trip ticket? (雙程票一張多少錢?) B: $750.00. (750 美元。)
有打折票嗎?	**Do you have a discount ticket?** A: Do you have a discount ticket? (有打折票嗎?) B: Sorry, there is no discount ticket at the moment. (對不起哦,暫時沒有。)
我想預定一張單程票。	**I´d like to reserve a one-way ticket.** A: I'd like to reserve a one-way ticket. (我想預定一張單程票。) B: Ok, wait for a minute. (好的,請稍等。)
您想訂頭等艙還是經濟艙的機票?	**You want to go first class or coach?** A: You want to go first class or coach? (您想訂頭等艙還是經濟艙的機票?) B: I prefer first class, what is the fare? (我想訂頭等艙的機票。多少錢?)
若取消我將通知您。	**I will notify you if there is cancellation.**

簽 證 Visa

我正在準備簽證面試。	**I am preparing for my visa interview.** A: I am preparing for my visa interview. (我正在準備簽證面試。) B: Good luck! (加油！)
護照拿到了嗎?	**Have you got your passport?** A: Have you got your passport? (護照拿到了嗎？) B: Yes, I got it last week. (嗯，我上個星期就已經拿到了。)
我的簽證下來了。	**I have been granted my visa.** A: I have been granted my visa. (我的簽證下來了。) B: So, when do you plan to go abroad? (那你打算什麼時候出國？)
我的簽證下個月就到期了。	**My visa will expire next month.** A: My visa will expire next month. (我的簽證下個月就到期了。) B: Are you going to extend your visa? (打算延期嗎？)
我的簽證可以延期嗎?	**Can I have my visa extended?** A: Can I have my visa extended? (我的簽證可以延期嗎?) B: Why not? (當然可以。) 注解 why not 的意思是"爲什麼不呢？"其實說直白點就是"當然可以"的意思。
我的簽證三個月有效。	**My visa is valid for 3 months.** A: My visa is valid for 3 months. (我的簽證三個月有效。) B: You should extend your visa if you want to stay longer in NY. (如果你想在紐約多呆一段時間，你應將簽證延期。)

體檢 & 檢疫 Physical & Quarantine

我明天去體檢。	**I'll have my physical checkup tomorrow.** A: Everything is ready except the physical checkup, right? (你所有的手續都辦好了,就差體檢了,是嗎?) B: Yes, I'll have my physical checkup tomorrow. (是的。我明天就去體檢。)
去體檢之前應該多喝水。	**You should drink more water before the physical checkup.** A: Do you have any suggestion? (你有什麼建議嗎?) B: You should drink more water before the physical checkup. (去體檢之前應該多喝水。)
體檢都包括哪些項目呢?	**What does the physical checkup include?** A: What does the physical checkup include? (體檢都包括哪些項目呢?) B: Including Examination of blood pressure, heartbeats, visual acuity, an X-ray , blood test and so on. (包括血壓、心跳、視力的檢查,拍 X 光片和驗血等等。)
我會提前打電話去預約,確認醫生是否在。	**I will call to make an appointment in advance to make sure that the doctors are available.**
通過體檢後,你會在一個月之內拿到你的護照。	**You will have your passport in a month after passing the physical checkup.**
我已經接種預防天花疫苗。	**I have been vaccinated against smallpox.**
你如果有動物制品或植物,一定要接受檢疫。	**If you have any animal products or plants, you must undergo a quarantine inspection.**

入 境 Immigration

我可以看一下護照嗎?	**May I see your passport, please?** A: May I see your passport, please? (我可以看一下護照嗎？) B: Here is my passport. / Here it is. (這是我的護照。)
出行的目的爲何?	**What´s the purpose of your visit?** 同 **What will you do here?** A: What's the purpose of your visit? (出行的目的爲何？) B: Sightseeing (Business). (觀光(公務)。)
預計在紐約停留多久?	**How long will you be staying in New York?** A: How long will you be staying in New York? (預計在紐約停留多久？) B: 5 days. (5 天。)
預計停留約 10 天。	**I plan to stay for about 10 days.** A: How long are you going to stay here? (您在此逗留多長時間？) B: I plan to stay for about 10 days. (預計停留約 10 天。) 
我祇是過境而已。	**I´m just passing through.** A: How long will you be staying in there? (你打算在那停留多長時間？) B: I'm just passing through. (我祇是過境而已。)
今晚即動身前往波士頓。	**I am leaving for Boston tonight.** A: When do you leave? (什麼時候出發？) B: I am leaving for Boston tonight. (今晚即動身前往波士頓。)
將在哪兒住宿?	**Where are you staying?**

是否有美國回程機票?

Do you have a return ticket to United States?

A: Do you have a return ticket to United States?
(是否有美國回程機票？)
B: Yes, here it is. (有的，這就是回程機票。)

隨身攜帶多少現金?

How much cash do you have with you?

A: How much cash do you have with you?
(隨身攜帶多少現金？)
B: I have about $800.00. (大約 800 元。)

好了，您可以通過了。

Ok, you´re through now.

A: Ok, you're through now. (好了，您可以通過了。)
B: Thanks. (謝謝。)

祝你玩得愉快。

Have a nice day.

A: Have a nice day. (祝你玩得愉快。)
B: Thank you. (謝謝。)

如入境時不適，則要即時向口岸衛生人員報告。

If felt sick at terminals, report to health inspection personnel immediately.

您可以到入境櫃臺去看看，可能還有部分店面開著。

There could be some shops open once you pass the immigration counter.

A: I need to buy something. (我想要買點東西。)
B: Oh, there could be some shops open once you pass the immigration counter. (哦，您可以到入境櫃臺去看看，可能還有部分店面開著。)

在入境移民服務區，乘客服務代表回答問題并且幫助人們排隊等候。

In the immigration area, the passenger service agent answer questions and help the people waiting in line.

A: Excuse me, do you know who can help me solve the problems?
(打擾一下，請問誰能幫我解决問題的呢？)
B: In the immigration area, the passenger service agent answer questions and help the people waiting in line. (在入境移民服務區，乘客服務代表回答問題并且幫助人們排隊等候。)

遺失行李 Lost Baggage

我在何處可取得行李?	**Where can I get my baggage?** A: Where can I get my baggage? (我在何處可取得行李?) B: You can get your baggage at Lost and Found Office. (你可以在行李遺失招領處把你的行李領回來。)
我找不到我的行李。	**I can´t find my baggage.** A: I can't find my baggage. (我找不到我的行李。) B: Please recall the place you lost your baggage. (請你回憶一下,你是在什麼地方丟失了行李?)
這是我的行李票。	**Here is my claim tag.** A: Take your baggage by claim tag. (憑票領回自己的行李。) B: Sir, here is my claim tag. (先生,這是我的行李票。)
是否可快速查詢一下?	**Could you please check it quickly?** A: Could you please check it quickly? (是否可快速查詢一下?) B: Ok, wait for a minute. (好的,請稍等。)
你能描述一下你的行李嗎?	**Can you describe your baggage?** A: Can you describe your baggage? (你能描述一下你的行李嗎?) B: It is a medium-sized Samsonite, and it's gray. (它是一個中型的灰色絲耐特皮箱。)
它是一個上面系有我名牌的大型皮制黑藍色行李箱。	**It is a large leather suitcase with my name tag. It´s dark blue.** A: Anything special about your baggage? (有什麼特別之處嗎?) B: It is a large leather suitcase with my name tag. It's dark blue. (它是一個上面系有我名牌的大型皮制黑藍色行李箱。)

我們正在調查，請稍等一下。	**Please wait for a moment while we are investigating.** A: How is it? Any result? (怎麼樣？有結果了嗎？) B: Please wait for a moment while we are investigating. (我們正在調查，請稍等一下。)
我們可能遺失了幾件行李，所以必須填份行李遺失報告。	**We may have lost some baggage so we´d like to make a lost baggage report.** A: We may have lost some baggage so we'd like to make a lost baggage report. (我們可能遺失了幾件行李，所以必須填份行李遺失報告。) B: No problem. (沒問題。)
多快可找到？	**How soon will I find out?** A: How soon will I find out? (多快能找到？) B: Before 6:00 pm today. (今天下午六點之前。)
一旦找到行李，請立即送到我停留的飯店。	**Please deliver the baggage to my hotel as soon as you´ve located it.** A: Please deliver the baggage to my hotel as soon as you've located it. (一旦找到行李，請立即送到我停留的飯店。) B: Ok, don't worry about it, sir. (好的，先生，請您放心。)
若是今天無法找到行李，你可如何幫助？	**How can you help me if you can´t find my baggage today?** A: How can you help me if you can't find my baggage today? (若是今天無法找到行李，你可如何幫助？) B: We will try our best to fix you up with a place to stay tonight and help you get your baggage back tomorrow. (我們會盡量幫您安排住的地方，明天一定能幫你把行李找回來。)
我想要購買過夜所需的用品。	**I´d like to purchase what I need for the night.** A: Is there anything we can help? (有什麼是我們能幫您的？) B: I'd like to purchase what I need for the night. (我想要購買過夜所需的用品。) 

海關申報 Customs Declaration

請出示護照和申報單。	**Your passport and declaration card, please.** A: Your passport and declaration card, please. (請出示護照和申報單。) B: Here are my passport and declaration card. (這是我的護照和申報單。)
是否有任何東西需要申報?	**Do you have anything to declare?** A: Do you have anything to declare? (是否有任何東西需要申報?) B: No, I don't. (沒有。) 
我所携帶的東西衹是一些自己的衣物、手提電腦和帶給我姐姐的禮物。	**The only things I brought were my own clothes, laptop and some gifts for my sister.**
請打開這個袋子。	**Please open this bag.** A: Please open this bag. (請打開這個袋子。) B: There are some gifts in the bag. (這袋子裏裝着的是一些禮物。)
這些是什麼?	**What are these?** A: What are these? Open this box, please. (這些是什麼? 請打開這個盒子。) B: Souvenir for my wife. (給我妻子的紀念品。)
這些是我私人使用的東西。	**These are for my personal use.** A: Are the pills for friends? (這些藥丸是帶給你朋友的嗎?) B: No. These are for my personal use. (不是,這些是我私人使用的。)
你能告訴我藥丸的成分嗎?	**Could you tell me the pills ingredients?**

這些是給朋友的禮物。	**These are gifts for my friends.** A: What is this thing for? (這些東西是做什麼用的？) B: These are gifts for my friends. (這些是給朋友的禮物。)
這些是我要帶去多倫多的紀念品。	**They are souvenirs that I´m taking to Toronto.** A: They are souvenirs that I'm taking to Toronto. (這些是我要帶去多倫多的紀念品。) B: I'm sorry. I'm afraid I'll have to check these. (對不起，恐怕我也得檢查一下。)
你有携帶任何酒類或香烟嗎?	**Do you have any liquor or cigarettes?** A: Do you have any liquor or cigarettes? (你有携帶任何酒類或香烟嗎？) B: Yes, I have two bottles of whisky. (是的，我帶了兩瓶威士忌。)
需要繳稅嗎?	**Is it taxable?** A: Is it taxable? (需要繳稅嗎？) B: No. It's OK. (不，不需要。)
這個相機是我私人使用的。	**The camera is for my personal use.** A: How many cameras do you bring? (你帶了多少臺相機？) B: Only one. It's for my personal use. (衹是帶了一臺，這個相機是我私人使用的。)
你必須爲這些物品繳付稅金。	**You´ll have to pay duty fee on them.** A: I have brought tobacco shred, perfumes and makeup. (我帶了烟絲、香水和化妝品。) B: You'll have to pay duty fee on them. (你必須爲這些物品繳付稅金。)
你還有其他行李嗎?	**Do you have any other baggage?**
好了！請將這張申報卡交給出口處的官員。	**Ok. Please give this declaration card to that officer at the exit.** A: Ok. Please give this declaration card to that officer at the exit. (好了！請將這張申報卡交給出口處的官員。) B: Thank you! (謝謝。)

機場旅游資訊 Airport Travel Information

旅游咨詢中心在哪裏?	**Where is the tourist information?** A: Where is the tourist information? (旅游咨詢中心在哪裏？) B: Go straight down the street and you will see it. (一直往前走就看到了。)
是否有機場巴士可到市區?	**Is there an airport bus to the city?** A: Is there an airport bus to the city? (是否有機場巴士可到市區？) B: Yes. This is the schedule. (有的。這是時刻表。) 
巴士站牌在哪裏?	**Where is the bus stop?** A: Excuse me, where is the bus stop? (打擾一下,巴士站牌在哪裏？) B: I'm looking for it, too. (我也正在找呢。)
我要如何才能到達希爾頓飯店?	**How can I get to Hilton Hotel?** A: How can I get to Hilton Hotel? (我要如何才能到達希爾頓飯店？) B: You can take the shuttle bus to there. (你可以搭乘到希爾頓飯店的接駁巴士。)
我在何處可搭乘希爾頓飯店的接駁巴士?	**Where can I get the shuttle bus for Hilton Hotel?** A: Where can I get the shuttle bus for Hilton Hotel? (我在何處可搭乘希爾頓飯店的接駁巴士？) B: There is a bus stop near the airport. (機場附近有接駁巴士的站牌。)
是否可提供我一份旅館的目録?	**Can I have a hotel list?** A: Can I have a hotel list? (是否可提供我一份旅館的目録？) B: Sure, here you are! (可以,給！)

我在哪裏可以拿到飯店目録呢?	**Where can I get a hotel list?** A: Where can I get a hotel list? (我在哪裏可以拿到飯店目録呢？) B: You can get it from the service counter over there. (你可以到服務臺那邊領取。)
是否可給我一份城市地圖?	**May I have a city map?** A: May I have a city map? (是否可給我一份城市地圖？) B: The big one or the small one? (你需要大的還是小的？)
我是否可在此預訂飯店?	**Can I reserve a hotel here?** A: Can I reserve a hotel here? (我是否可在此預訂飯店？) B: Yes, you can. Which hotel would you like to reserve? (可以，請問你想訂哪家飯店？)
是否可以建議一間較爲廉價的旅館?	**Can you recommend a hotel which is not too expensive?** A: Can you recommend a hotel which is not too expensive? (是否可以建議一間較爲廉價的旅館？) B: Do you have any requirements? (您有什麽要求？)
有没有每晚花費在 80 美元以下的飯店?	**Is there a hotel which costs under 80 dollars a night?** A: Is there a hotel which costs under 80 dollars a night? (有没有每晚花費在 80 美元以下的飯店？) B: Yes, there are several hotels costs under 80 dollars a night. (有的，有幾家飯店每晚花費都在 80 美元以下。)
是否可建議一家位于市中心的旅館?	**Could you recommend a hotel in the city center?** A: Could you recommend a hotel in the city center? (是否可建議一家位于市中心的旅館？) B: Which one do you prefer? The luxurious one or the simple one? (您需要豪華型的還是簡約型的？)
我想要住在靠近車站(海灘)的飯店。	**I´d like to stay at a hotel near the station (beach).**

每晚費用爲多少?

How much is it per night?

A: How much is it per night? (每晚費用爲多少？)
B: $60.00. (60 美元。)

費用是否包含稅與服務費?

Does it include tax and service charge?

A: Does it include tax and service charge?
(費用是否包含稅與服務費？)
B: Yes, they are all included. (是的，已經全部包括了。)

早餐是否已包含于費用內?

Is breakfast included?

A: Is breakfast included? (早餐是否已包含于費用內？)
B: Exclusive of breakfast. (不包含在內。)

若停留數日是否有任何折扣?

Is there a discount for staying several days?

A: Is there a discount for staying several days?
(若停留數日是否有任何折扣？)
B: If you stay over two days, we can give you 10% off.
(如果停留兩天以上，我們可以給你打九折。)

我想要停留三晚。

I´d like to stay for three nights.

A: How long are you going to stay here?
(你想停留多長時間？)
B: I'd like to stay for three nights. (我想停留三晚。)

這城市有什麼景點嗎?

Is there anything interesting in this city?

A: Is there anything interesting in this city?
(這城市有什麼景點嗎？)
B: We have a beautiful natural park.
(這裏有一座美麗的自然公園。)

這城市什麼出名?

What´s this city famous for?

A: What's this city famous for? (這城市什麼出名？)
B: Tea and silk. (茶和絲綢。)

推薦一些地方去參觀好嗎?

Would you recommend some places for sightseeing?

A: Would you recommend some places for sightseeing?
(推薦幾個觀光的好去處好嗎？)
B: How about Great Canyon? (大裂谷怎麼樣？)

機位查詢、確認 Confirm the Reservation

聯合航空,您好。

Hello. This is United Airlines.

A: Hello. This is United Airlines. (聯合航空,您好!)
B: Hello. I'd like to reconfirm my flight.
(您好,我想確認一下我的班機。)

請說您的名字與班機號碼?

What´s your name and flight number?

A: What's your name and flight number?
(請說您的名字與班機號碼?)
B: My name is Jerry, and the flight number is UA 003 for Los Angeles. (我的名字是杰瑞,班機號碼是飛往洛杉機的聯合航空 003 班機。)

行程是哪一天?

When is it?

A: When is it? (行程是哪一天?)
B: June 10th. (6 月 10 日。)

我找不到您的名字。

I can´t find your name.

A: I can't find your name. (我找不到您的名字。)
B: Really? (真的?)

我仍然無法在訂位名單中找到您的名字。

I still can´t find your name on the reservation list.

A: I still can't find your name on the reservation list.
(我仍然無法在訂位名單中找到您的名字。)
B: Then, please give me a new reservation.
(那麼,請幫我重新訂位。)

頭等艙已經訂完了,但是商務艙還有一些空位。

First class is full, but there are still seats in business class.

你何時開始辦理登機手續?

What time do you start check-in?

你必須在至少1小時前辦理登機。	**You must check–in at least one hour before.** A: What time am I supposed to check in? (我應該什麼時候去辦理登機手續？) B: You must check-in at least one hour before. (你必須在至少 1 小時前辦理登機。)
抱歉,這班飛機已客滿。	**Sorry, this flight is full.** A: I want to make a change. Please cancel this flight and transfer me to flight A005. (現在我想更改我的預約，請取消這個預訂改成 A005 航班。) B: Sorry, this flight is full. (抱歉,這班飛機已客滿。)
下一班飛往洛杉機的班機何時起飛?	**When will the next flight to Los Angeles leave?** A: When will the next flight to Los Angeles leave? (下一班飛往洛杉機的班機何時起飛？) B: Four hours later. (四個小時後。)
太好了。請告訴我班機號碼與起飛時間?	**That will be fine. What´s the flight number and departure time?** A: That will be fine. What's the flight number and departure time? (太好了。請告訴我班機號碼與起飛時間？) B: The flight number is A006, and the departure time is 3:10p.m.. (班機號碼是 A006,起飛時間是下午三點十分。)
我想要確認班機時間沒有改變。	**I´d like to make sure of the time it leaves.** A: I'd like to make sure of the time it leaves. (我想要確認班機時間沒有改變。) B: May I have your name again? (請再告訴我一次您的名字？)
別擔心，這班班機仍有空位提供新的訂位者。	**Anyway, we have seats for new bookings on this flight. No problem.**
您已完成訂位了。	**Now you have been booked.**
若是我在此等候，有機位的機率有多大?	**What is the possibility of getting a seat if I wait?**

機場用語 At the Airport

去倫敦的航班多長時間一班?	How often is there a flight to London?
下一班去華盛頓的飛機幾點起飛?	At what time does the next plane to Washington leave?
它們是直達班機嗎?	Are they non-stop flights?
我可以預定去紐約的8號班機座位嗎?	Could I make a reservation for flight 8 to New York?
從西雅圖到紐約要飛多久?	How long is the flight from Seattle to New York?
這裏是去東京的MU562航班的登記處嗎?	Is this where I have to check in for Flight MU562 to Tokyo?
星期天有去香港的班機嗎?	Are there any planes to HongKong Sunday?
你可以告訴我該走哪條通道嗎?	Do you know which channel to go through?
來回的票要多少錢?	How much is the round trip ticket?
我們每小時都有去巴黎的班機。	We have flights to Paris every hour.
請出示機票和護照好嗎?	May I have your ticket and passport?
是否有機場費要付?	Is there any airport fees that I have to pay?

請把您的行李放在秤上。	Please put your bags on the scales.
如果你有東西需要申報，請走紅色通道。	You can go through the red channel if you have anything to declare.
請帶我去肯尼迪國際機場。	Please take me to JFK international airport.
請帶我到國際航班出港航區。	Please take me to the international departure terminal.
請問 25 號登機口在哪裏?	Can you tell me where is departure gate 25?
請問我的航班的起飛時間是多少?	What is the departure time of my flight?
美國航空公司的 F32 航班已經延誤了。	American Airline Flight Number F32 has been delayed!

搭乘西北航空公司 G88 航班的旅客，現在可以開始辦理登機手續!	Passengers for NorthWest Airline Flight Number G88 can check in now!
請給我看你的登機牌。	Please show me your boarding pass.
請問你有幾件行李要托運?	How many luggages you would like to check in?
請問我可以托運幾件行李?	How many luggages am I allowed to checked in?
請問，你是否要將這些行李，一直托運到你的目的地?	Are you checking these luggages all the way to the destination?
我有一件隨身携帶的行李。	I have one carry-on luggage.

住宿 Staying in A Hotel

我會晚一點到達，請保留所預訂的房間。	**I'll arrive late. Please keep my reservation.** A: Hello, sir. The room you have reserved will expire in 15 minutes. Do you need to cancel the reservation? (先生，您好！您所預定的房間還有十五分鐘就過期了，請問您需要取消預定嗎？) B: I'll arrive late. Please keep my reservation. (我會晚一點到達，請保留所預訂的房間。)
我在曼谷已預訂了房間。	**I made a reservation in Bangkok.** A: Have you made the reservation? (你訂房間了嗎？) B: I made a reservation in Bangkok. (我在曼谷已預訂了房間。)
我的名字是琳達。	**My name is Linda.** A: Your name, please. (你的名字，謝謝！) B: My name is Linda. (我的名字是琳達。)
我想要一間安靜一點的房間。	**I'd like a quiet room.** A: What kind of room do you like? (你想要什麼樣的房間？) B: I'd like a quiet room. (我想要一間安靜一點的房間。)
我想要樓上的房間。	**I'd like a room on the upper level.** A: How about a room on the first floor? (一樓的房間可以嗎？) B: I'd like a room on the upper level. (我想要樓上的房間。) 
我想要一間有陽臺的房間。	**I prefer a room with a balcony.** A: What kind of room would you prefer? (你喜歡什麼樣的房間？) B: I prefer a room with a balcony. (我想要一間有陽臺的房間。)

我可以看一看房間嗎?	**May I see the room?** A: May I see the room? (我可以看一看房間嗎?) B: Certainly, sir. This way, please! (當然可以,先生,這邊請!)
是否還有更大的(更好的/更便宜的)房間?	**Do you have any rooms bigger (better / cheaper)?** A: Do you have any rooms cheaper? (是否還有更便宜的房間?) B: I'm sorry. This is the cheapest one. (抱歉,這已經是最便宜的了。) 
我要訂這間房間。	**I'll take this room.** A: I'll take this room. (我要訂這間房間。) B: Ok, May I have your ID card, please? (好的,請出示您的身份證,謝謝!)
麻煩填寫這張住宿登記表。	**Would you fill in this registration form?** A: I will check-in tonight. (我今晚入住這個房間。) B: Ok. Would you fill in this registration form? (麻煩填寫這張住宿登記表。)
這裏可使用旅行支票嗎?	**Do you accept traveler´s checks?** A: Do you accept traveler's checks? (這裏可使用旅行支票嗎?) B: Sorry, sir. You can only pay in cash or by credit card here. (先生,不好意思,我們這裏衹可以用現金或者信用卡付賬。)
是否可代爲保管貴重物品?	**Could you keep my valuables?** A: Could you keep my valuables? (是否可代爲保管貴重物品?) B: You can deposit your valuables in the hotel safe. (你可以存放你的貴重物品在旅館的保險箱裏。)
是否可在此購買觀光巴士券?	**Can I get a ticket for the sightseeing bus here?** A: Can I get a ticket for the sightseeing bus here? (是否可在此購買觀光巴士券?) B: Yes, you can get it at the hotel reception. (可以,請你在服務臺處購買。)

旅館內有美容院嗎?	**Is there a beauty salon?** A: Is there a beauty salon? (旅館內有美容院嗎?) B: Yes. There is a leisure and entertainment area on the fifth floor. (有的,五樓是休閑娛樂區。)
是否可給我一張有旅館地址的名片?	**Can I have a card with the hotel´s address?** A: Can I have a card with the hotel's address? (是否可給我一張有旅館地址的名片?) B: Yes, here you are. (可以,這是我們旅館的名片。)
最近的地鐵站在哪裏?	**Where is the nearest subway station?** A: Where is the nearest subway station? (最近的地鐵站在哪裏?) B: Go right when you leave the hotel. About 10 minutes walk. (出旅館向右走,大概走 10 分鐘就到。)
何時需退房?	**When is check out time?** A: When is check out time? (何時需退房?) B: Our check out time is 11 a.m.. (我們的退房時間是上午 11 點。)
明早你是否能幫我將行李拿到大廳?	**Could you bring my baggage down to the lobby tomorrow morning?** A: Could you bring my baggage down to the lobby tomorrow morning? (明早你是否能幫我將行李拿到大廳?) B: Sure. What time are you leaving? (當然。你何時離開?) 
我八點鐘離開。	**I leave at 8 o´clock.** A: I leave at 8 o'clock. (我八點鐘離開。) B: Then I'll go to your room at 7:50. (那麼,我將在 7 點 50 分到你的房間。)
這是 316 號房。我想要一件毛毯。	**This is room 316. I´d like a blanket, please.** A: Hello, may I help you? (您好,請問有什麼可以幫您?) B: This is room 316. I'd like a blanket, please. (這是 316 號房。我想要一件毛毯。)

我總共有3件行李。	**I have three pieces of baggage.** A: I have three pieces of baggage. (我總共有3件行李。) B: Please leave them outside your room tomorrow morning. (明早,請將行李放在你的門口。)
請送一壺咖啡給我。	**Please bring me a pot of coffee.** A: Please bring me a pot of coffee. (請送一壺咖啡給我。) B: Do you want it cold or hot? (要冰的還是熱的?)
請送給我一些冰塊和水。	**Please bring me some ice cubes and water.** A: Please bring me some ice cubes and water. (請送給我一些冰塊和水。) B: Which room do you live in? (請問你在哪個房間?)
我想設定早晨的呼叫鈴。	**I´d like a morning call, please.** A: I'd like a morning call, please. (我想設定早晨的呼叫鈴。) B: What time? (幾點?) 
空調(電視、燈)無法開啓。	**The air–conditioner (T.V. set、light) doesn´t work.** A: The air-conditioner doesn't work. (我房間的空調壞了。) B: Just a second, please. We will deal with it immediately. (請稍等一會,我們馬上去處理。)
熱水不够熱。	**The hot water is not hot enough.**
我住得很愉快。	**I enjoy my stay.**
我有些衣服需要送洗。	**I have some laundry.**
這些衣服需要熨。	**I´d like these clothes ironed.**
請將你需要洗的衣服放在紙袋中,并將衣物内容寫下來。	**Please put your laundry in the paper bag and write down the contents of the laundry on it.**

房間內沒有熱水。	**There is no hot water.**
明天（後天）是否可洗好？	**Will it be ready by tomorrow (the day after tomorrow)?**
我今晚(明天)就要。	**I need them tonight (tomorrow).**
我明早 9 點以前需要這些清洗的衣物。	**I´d like to have my laundry by 9 o´clock tomorrow morning.**
這件不是我的。	**This is not mine.**
有一件遺失了。	**There´s one piece missing.**
明早幾時開始可以送洗衣物？	**From what time do you accept laundry tomorrow morning?** A: From what time do you accept laundry tomorrow morning? (明早幾時開始可以送洗衣物？) B: From 9 a.m. to 4 p.m.. (從早上 9 點開始到下午 4 點爲止。)
旅館中有理發廳嗎？	**Is there a barber shop in this hotel?**
我想要預約今天下午 5 點。	**I´d like to make an appointment for 5 p.m. today.**
本酒店提供保險櫃。	**The hotel provides safe deposit boxes.**
我要退房。請給我帳單。	**I´d like to check out. My bill, please.** A: I'd like to check out. My bill, please. (我要退房。請給我帳單。) B: Here is your bill. The total is $180.00. (這是您的賬單，總額是 180 美元.) 
我想用信用卡付帳。	**I want to pay by credit card.** A: How would you like to pay, by cash or by credit card? (請問您用現金付賬還是信用卡付賬？) B: I want to pay by credit card. (我想用信用卡付帳。)

用 餐 In A Restaurant

餐廳在哪兒?	**Where is the dining room?** A: Where is the dining room? (餐廳在哪兒?) B: On the second floor. (在二樓。)
餐廳幾點開始營業?	**What time does the dining room open?** A: What time does the dining room open? (餐廳幾點開始營業?) B: The restaurant opens at 10 a.m.. (早上十點開始營業。)
早餐幾點開始供應?	**What time can I have breakfast?** A: What time can I have breakfast? (早餐幾點開始供應?) B: Breakfast will be served from 7:00 a.m. to 10:00 p.m.. (早餐供應時間是 7:00-10:00。)
這附近您能推薦家好吃的飯館嗎?	**Could you recommend a good restaurant near here?** A: Could you recommend a good restaurant near here? (這附近您能推薦家好吃的飯館嗎?) B: What kind of food do you like? (您最想吃什麽菜呢?) 注解 recommend "推薦,建議"。
我想吃意大利菜。	**I´d like some Italian food.** A: I'd like some Italian food. (我想吃意大利菜。) B: I know a great Italian restaurant nearby. (我知道這附近有家很不錯的意大利餐館。)
這附近有没有還在營業的飯館?	**Are there any restaurants still open near here?** A: Are there any restaurants still open near here? (這附近有没有還在營業的飯館?) B: It's late. Many restaurants are closed. (現在已經很晚了,很多餐館都打烊了。)

這附近有中式餐館嗎?

Is there a Chinese restaurant around here?

A: Is there a Chinese restaurant around here?
(這附近有中式餐館嗎?)
B: Yes, there's one. (是的,有一家。)

我想訂餐。今天晚上7點,6個人的位子。

I´d like to make a reservation for six people at seven o´clock tonight.

A: Hello, this is the Park Restaurant. May I help you?
(您好,這是公園餐廳。我可以爲您服務嗎?)
B: I'd like to make a reservation for six people at seven o'clock tonight.
(我想訂餐。今天晚上7點,6個人的位子。)

對不起,今天晚上都訂滿了。

I´m sorry. We´re all booked up tonight.
同 I´m sorry. We are quite full tonight.
I´m sorry, all the tables are booked tonight.

注解 用 booked up 或 booked 來表示"訂滿了"。

要等多長時間?

How long do we have to wait?

我們可以等。

We can wait.

一頓飯多少錢?

What is the price of a dinner?

可以預訂幾點的?

What time can we make a reservation?

注解 make a reservation "預訂"。

一直營業到幾點?

How late are you open?

A: How late are you open? (一直開到幾點?)
B: Until eleven. (到11點。)

注解 How late...? 表示"……到幾點?"

衣着上有什麼規定嗎?

What is your dress code?

A: What is your dress code? (服裝上有什麼規定?)
B: We require a jacket and tie. (要求穿外衣、打領帶。)

注解 code "規定,規範"。

女性必須穿禮服嗎?

Should the ladies wear dresses?

我必須得穿外衣打領帶嗎?	**Should I wear a jacket and tie?** 注解 Should... "必須、應該……嗎?"。
請問您幾位?	**How many in your party(group)?** A: How many in your party? (請問您幾位?) B: Four. (四個人。) 注解 這裏的 party 不表示"聚會",而表示"一行人,一群人"。
我們需要一張大桌子。	**We need a large table, please.**
對不起,我想取消訂餐。	**I´m sorry, but I have to cancel my reservation.**
請給我菜單。	**Could I have a menu, please?** **May I see your menu, please?** **I´d like to see a menu, please.**
有中文的菜單嗎?	**Do you have a menu in Chinese?**
請給我看一下酒單。	**May I see the wine list, please?**
你們都有些什麼酒?	**What kind of wine do you have available?**
您來點兒什麼?	**May I take your order?** A: May I take your order? (您來點兒什麼?) B: Well, let's see... (唔,讓我想想……)
可以點菜了嗎?	**Are you ready to order?**
有什麼菜可以推薦的嗎?	**What do you recommend?** A: What do you recommend? (有什麼菜可以推薦的嗎?) B: The seafood is good here. (我們店的海鮮很可口。)
我要一份牛排。	**I´d like a steak.** A: I'd like a steak. (我要一份牛排。) B: How would you like it done? (要幾成熟的?) 注解 rare "三成熟(中嫩的)", medium "適中的,半成熟", well-done "烤得熟的,八成熟"。

我想要和那個一樣的。	**Can I have the same as that?** A: Can I have the same as that? (我想要和那個一樣的。) B: Sure, no problem. (好的,沒問題。)
您這兒有什麼地方風味嗎?	**Do you have any local specialties?** 注解 local "這一地區的", specialty "特色,特產"。
我要一個 70 美元的晚餐包括酒水。	**I´d like to have dinner for seventy dollars including drinks.** 注解 including..."包含……"。
請做得清淡點。	**Please make it light.**
我要紅葡萄酒。	**I´d like some red wine, please.**
您用早餐嗎?	**Are you having breakfast?** A: Are you having breakfast? (您用早餐嗎?) B: No, I'll just have a cup of coffee. (不,我衹要一杯咖啡。)
還要別的嗎?	**Anything else?** A: Anything else? (還要別的嗎?) B: No, thank you. That's all. (不要了,就要這些吧,謝謝。)
套餐裏包括咖啡嗎?	**Is coffee included with this meal?**
我沒有點這個菜。	**I didn´t order this.** A: I didn't order this. (我沒有點這個菜。) B: You didn't, sir? (您沒要嗎?)
這和我點的不一樣。	**This is not what I ordered.**
我點的菜還沒上。	**My order hasn´t come yet.** 注解 order 是名詞,表示"訂的東西"、"訂購物品"。
這個好吃嗎?	**Is this delicious?** 同 **Does this taste good?**

好吃。	**It´s good.** ▣ **It´s delicious.** 注解 Good 和 delicious 都是表示好吃的意思。而 It's not good. It doesn't taste good. 則爲"不好吃。"的意思。
看上去真好吃!	**This looks great!**
我都要流口水了!	**My mouth is watering.**

味道很怪。	**This tastes strange.**
我什麼都不想吃。	**I don´t feel like eating anything.** 注解 feel like... "產生想要(飲食等)的感覺"。
我很能喝。	**I drink like a fish.**
我酒量小。	**I get drunk easily.**
我酒量還可以。	**I can hold my own.** 注解 hold my own 表示 "一般"、"比賽等中不輸"、"不亞于任何人"。
我能喝很多酒。	**I can drink a lot.** ▣ **I´m a strong drinker.**
請把鹽遞給我。	**Please pass me the salt.** 注解 pass 在飯桌上"傳遞,遞過來"。
這是餃子。	**It´s called dumpling.**
你可以沾醬油。	**You can dip it in soy sauce.** ▣ **Place the sushi in some soy sauce.** A: How do you eat sushi? (壽司怎麼吃呀?) B: You can dip it in soy sauce. (你可以沾醬油。) 注解 dip 表示"浸泡或塗抹液體"。
你會用筷子嗎?	**Can you use chopsticks?**
這咖啡不够熱。	**This coffee is not hot enough.**

好美味啊！這是什麽菜？	**These are delicious! What are they?** A: These are delicious! What are they? (好美味啊！這是什麽菜？) B: Oh, that's cauliflower. (哦，這是花椰菜。)
面包烤焦了。	**This bread is burned.** 注解 soggy "面包等没有烤透的"狀態。
這牛肉不新鮮了。	**The beef is stale.** 注解 stale 也可用來表示面包等"不新鮮"、"走味"、"有霉味的"。
你想要清咖啡呢還是要加牛奶？	**Do you want black coffee or coffee with milk?** A: Do you want black coffee or coffee with milk? (你想要清咖啡呢還是要加牛奶？) B: I prefer the black coffee. (我比較喜歡喝清咖啡。)
這咖啡太苦了。	**This coffee tastes bitter.**
這牛奶酸了。	**This milk is sour.**

這肉太老。	**This meat is tough.** 注解 Tough 表示"硬"的意思。如果説"This meat is tender."則表示"這肉挺嫩。"
這湯太濃了。	**This soup is too heavy.** 注解 heavy 可表示味道重。如果要表示味道淡可以用 light。
這道菜太咸了。	**The dish is too salty.**
太油膩。	**It´s too greasy.**
太燙了。	**It´s too hot.**
這食物有點辣。	**The food is a bit hot.**
我的筷子掉了。	**I dropped my chopsticks.**

幹辣椒使我的嘴都麻了。	**The chili burned my mouth.** 注解（吃了辣椒或芥末等辛辣的東西時。）burn 除了"燃燒"、"燒焦"以外，還有"嘴和舌頭都麻木了"的意思。
我吃飽了。	**I´m very full.**
我已經吃得够多了。	**I´ve had enough.**
你也來點兒嗎?	**Would you like some?** A: Would you like some? (你也來點兒嗎？) B: Yes, please. (好吧。)
再喝一杯嗎?	**Would you like another drink?** A: Would you like another drink? (再喝一杯嗎？) B: No, I think I've had enough. (不，我喝得够多的了。)
請結賬。	**Bill, please.** 同 **I´d like the check, please.**
我請客。	**It´s on me.** 同 **This is my treat.** **I´ll pay for dinner.** **I´ll treat you.** A: It's on me. (我請客。) B: Oh, you're so kind. Thank you. (哦！你真大方，謝謝！)
我們各付各的吧。	**Let´s go Dutch.** 同 **Let´s split the bill. / Let´s divide the cost.** 注解 Dutch 表示"荷蘭人"，而 go Dutch 則表示"自己的費用自己付"、"分攤"。
我覺得這兒算錯了。	**I´m afraid there is a mistake here.** A: I'm afraid there is a mistake here. (我覺得這兒算錯了。) B: Let me have a look. (讓我看一下！) 注解 I'm afraid... "我覺得是不是……"，一般用于不太好的事情。mistake 表示"錯誤"。
不用找錢了。	**Keep the change.**

觀 光 Sightseeing

能告訴我這座城市有哪些好玩的地方嗎?	**Please tell me about some interesting places in this town.**
這兒有沒有可看的地方?	**Is there anything to visit here?**
博物館幾點開館?	**When does the museum open?** 注解 When does the museum close? (博物館幾點閉館?)
我對建築感興趣。	**I´m interested in architecture.** A: What are you interested in? (你對什麼感興趣?) B: I'm interested in architecture. (我對建築感興趣。)
都有哪些路綫的旅行呢?	**What kind of tours do you have?** 同 **What kind of tours are available?** **What kind of tours do you offer?** **What kind of tours are there?**
請告訴我去的路綫。	**Please show me the way.**
他們星期六開門嗎?	**Are they open on Saturday?**
有旅游車嗎?	**Are there any sightseeing buses?**
我想坐出租車旅游。	**I´d like a tour by taxi.**
我們可以要一位中文導游嗎?	**Could we have a Chinese–speaking tour guide?**
入場券多少錢?	**How much is the entrance fee?**
那個建築物是什麼?	**What´s that building?**

它的歷史有多久?	**How old is it?**
這個古迹有個美麗的傳說。	**This historical site has a beautiful story.**
我們能進到裏面嗎?	**Can we go in?** A: Can we go in? (我們能進到裏面嗎?) B: Of course. (當然能。)
我們去看看那座城堡吧。	**Let´s go to see the castle.**
多美的景色呀!	**What a beautiful view!**
我想多呆一會兒。	**I want to stay longer.** A: Let's leave now. (我們走吧!) B: I want to stay longer. (我多呆一會兒。)
這兒可以照相嗎?	**May I take a picture here?**
您能給我們照張相嗎?	**Would you take a picture for us?**
哪兒有禮品店?	**Where is the gift shop?**
這裏有什麼地方特產嗎?	**Are there some special local products here?**
今天晚上的節目是什麼?	**What´s on tonight?** 注解 on 除了表示"在……之上"之外,還有類似"電影上映,戲劇上演"的意思。
一共演多長時間?	**How long does it last?** 注解 last 有表示"連續,持續"的意思。
我還有許多地方要去參觀。	**I have many places to visit.** A: I have many places to visit. (我還有許多地方要去參觀。) B: I'll accompany you. (我陪你去。)

Moods
【情　緒】

- 高　興
- 驚　訝
- 感　動
- 自　信
- 無　聊
- 生　氣
- 爲　難
- 害　羞
- 難　過

高 興 Happy

通過面試我高興極了。	**I´m extremely happy that I have passed the interview.** 回 **I feel quite happy that I have passed the interview.** A: What are you looking so pleased about? (什麼事使你這麼高興？) B: I'm extremely happy that I have passed the interview. (通過面試我高興極了。) 注解 happy 可以用 extremely, particularly, heavenly, quite 等修飾，表示特別，極其高興。
你今天看起來很高興。	**You look very happy today.** 回 **You seem very happy today.** **You look cheerful today.** A: You look very happy today. (你今天看起來很高興。) B: I got promoted. (我升職了。)
什麼事值得這麼高興？	**What calls for this merriment?** A: What calls for this merriment? (什麼事值得這麼高興？) B: I got a salary raise. (我加薪了。) 
媽媽面帶喜色。	**Mother has a happy look on her face.** 回 **Mother wears a happy expression.** A: Mother has a happy look on her face. What's the good news? (媽媽面帶喜色。有什麼好事？) B: I don't know. (不知道哦！) 注解 have a happy look on one's face 和 wear a happy expression 都是面帶喜色的意思。
我對一切都滿意。	**I´m happy about everything.** A: How's your new job? (你的新工作怎樣？) B: I'm happy about everything. (我對一切都滿意。)

這消息真令我高興。	**The news made me happy.** **同 The news rendered me happy.** A: We'll have a trip next month. (我們下個月去旅游。) B: Really? The news made me happy. (真的嗎? 這消息真令我高興。)
我們在一起很快樂。	**We are happy together.** A: We are happy together. (我們在一起很快樂。) B: We shall get together often in the future. (以後我們要經常聚聚。)
瞧他們那高興勁兒。	**See how happy they look.** A: See how happy they look. (瞧他們那高興勁兒。) B: They haven't seen each other for a long time. (他們好久沒見了。)
爲什麼那麼高興?	**Why are you so happy?** A: Why are you so happy? (爲什麼那麼高興?) B: I'm going to get married. (我很快要結婚了。)
我好興奮啊。	**I´m ecstatic.** A: I won the lottery! I'm ecstatic. (我中獎了。我好興奮啊。) B: Congratulations. (恭喜恭喜。) 注解 也可以說 I'm excited. 但是 excited 沒有 ecstatic 的程度那麼深，ecstatic 有狂喜的意思。
我太激動了。	**I´m thrilled.** A: We're having a baby. (我們有孩子了。) B: Great! I'm thrilled. (太好了! 我太激動了。)
我感到非常愉快。	**I feel like a million dollars.** A: How did you spend your holiday? (假期過得怎樣?) B: I feel like a million dollars. (我感到非常愉快。)
我今天的心情很好。	**I´m in a good mood today.** A: I'm in a good mood today. (我今天的心情很好。) B: Any good things happened? (有什麼好事發生?)

我好像到了天堂。

I´m in heaven.

A: Did she agree to be your girlfriend?
(她答應做你女朋友了？)
B: Yeah. I'm in heaven. (是啊。我好像到了天堂。)

我從沒有這麼高興過。

I´ve never been this happy.

I´ve never been as happy as I am now.
This is the happiest moment in my life.
This is the best moment of my life.
I couldn´t be happier.

我興奮得飄飄然。

I am walking on air.

A: I am walking on air. (我興奮得飄飄然。)
B: You have passed the exam? (你通過考試了？)

注解 walk on air 是習慣用語。

沒有比這更讓人高興的了。

Nothing could be more wonderful.

Nothing would please me more.
Nothing could be nicer.

你使我感覺到了幸福。

You made me happy.

A: Baby, have you got the present?
(寶貝，收到禮物了嗎？)
B: Yeah. Thank you. You made me happy.
(收到了，謝謝。你使我感覺到了幸福。)

今天的運氣真好。

I lucked out today.

I was lucky today.
Today´s my lucky day.
I feel lucky today.

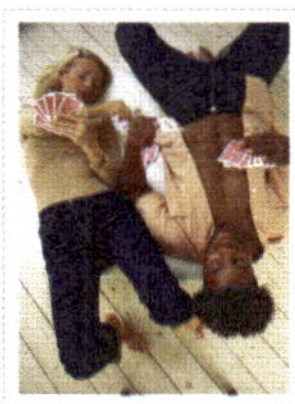

A: You win again. (你又贏了。)
B: I lucked out today. (今天的運氣真好。)

難以相信。

It´s unbelievable.

Unbelievable. / It´s hard to believe.
Incredible.

A: You made it, good deal! (你成功了，太棒了！)
B: It's unbelievable. (難以相信。)

你真走運。	**It´s your lucky day.** A: I found $100.00 on the street. (我在街上揀了 100 美元。) B: It's your lucky day. (你真走運。)
怎麼一直在笑?	**Why do you keep smiling?** A: Why do you keep smiling? (怎麼一直在笑?) B: I'm looking forward to the gathering tonight. (我期待着今晚的聚會。)
事情進行得比我們想象的順利。	**Things go more smoothly than we imagined.** A: Things go more smoothly than we imagined. (事情進行得比我們想象的順利。) B: I'm glad to hear that. (聽到這個很開心。)
我太興奮了,睡不着。	**I am too excited to go to sleep.** A: Why don't you go to sleep? (你怎麼還不睡?) B: I am too excited to go to sleep. (我太興奮了,睡不着。) 
太棒了!	**Bravo!** 同 **How wonderful. / Fantastic! / Terrific!** **Just wonderful! / It was really neat!** **Sounds wonderful! / Excellent.** A: We got the first prize. (我們得了第一名。) B: Bravo! (太棒了!)
太好了!	**Splendid!** 同 **How nice! / Very good.** **That would be lovely. / That sounds great.** A: My experiment was a success! (我的實驗成功了。) B: Splendid! (太好了。)
簡直不敢相信。	**Too good to be true.** A: This is your admission notice of Harvard University. (這是你的哈佛大學録取通知書。) B: Too good to be true. (簡直不敢相信。)

驚 訝 Surprise

真沒想到。	**What a surprise.** A: What a surprise meeting you here. (真沒想到在這裏見到你。) B: Oh, it's you. I'm so glad to see you. (噢，是你。好開心見到你。)
太驚人了。	**How amazing.** 回 **How surprising.**
這真是不可思議。	**It is truly unbelievable.**
真想不到！	**How about that!** 回 **Imagine that!** **Fancy that!** **Well, shut my mouth!**
我簡直不能相信自己的眼睛。	**I just could not believe my eyes.**
不可能。	**It can´t be.**
你在和我開玩笑吧？	**Are you kidding me?** 回 **Are you joking with me?**
天啊！	**Good heavens!** 回 **My god.** **Oh, god!** **Oh, my goodness!** **Oh, dear!** 
你相信嗎？	**Can you believe it?**
居然有這樣的事？	**Have such thing unexpectedly?**

感 動 Moved

我爲之深深感動。	I am profoundly touched. 回 I am deeply touched. I am deeply moved. I am extremely moved. I am greatly touched.  注解 touched 和 moved 可以互相替换,都表示感动。
我好感動。	I am moved.
我感動得流泪。	I was moved to tears. 注解 be moved to tears:感动得流泪。
那個故事深深地感動了我。	The story affected me deeply.
我聽了他的話很受感動。	I was deeply affected by his words.
我看了表演深受感動。	I was deeply affected by the performance.
他們似乎很感動。	They seem to be moved.
他的信很感人。	His letter was touching.
太感人了!	Impressive! 回 It´s really touching!
這情景很感人。	The sight is quite moving.
我快哭了。	I´m almost crying.
他打動了我的心。	He touched my heart.

自信 Confident

我對自己有信心。	I have confidence in myself.
我相信自己可以做到。	I believe I can do it.
沒問題。	Most assuredly I can. No sweat. No problem.
這我是有信心的。	I am confident of this.
我們一定會成功。	It is certain that we shall succeed.
我有把握能贏得比賽。	I´m sure of winning the game.
我絕對有把握。	I am dead sure.
相信我。	Believe me. Trust me. Count on me.
我自己可以應付。	I can deal with it by myself.
我會有辦法的。	I´ll find a way.
總有辦法可以解決問題的。	There are always ways to fix that.
我們可以解決這個問題。	We can work it out.
我不會讓你失望的。	I won´t let you down.
交給我吧。	Just leave it to me.

無 聊 Boring

他很無趣。	He is lame. 回 He is dull.
這份工作快讓我無聊死了。	This work is boring me to death.
我們的假日過得好無聊，每天都下雨。	We had a mouldy holiday – it rained every day.
這游戲已經讓我覺得無聊了。	I get tired of this game. 注解 get tired of something. / somebody. 對某人或某事感到厭倦。
這本小説無聊得讓我昏昏欲睡。	This novel is so dry that it makes me want to sleep.
那個講座太無聊了，我整個過程都在睡覺。	The lecture was so dull that I slept right through it.
那個教授講課無聊透頂。	That professor gives very boring classes.
我沒事做。	I have nothing to do.
每天都一樣。	One day is just like the next.
生活真無趣。	Life is boring.
我閑得發慌。	Time hangs heavy on my hands.
我晚上閑着無事很無聊。	I have no fun in spending the evening doing nothing.
今天我很閑。	I am very free today.

生 氣 Angry

我很生氣。	I fly into a rage. 回 I became very angry.
我生氣了。	I got into a temper.
我要氣瘋了。	I got mad.
我很惱火。	I am very annoyed.
那使我火冒三丈。	That made me savage.
我還在生氣。	I´m still angry.
我對你生氣。	I was offended with you.
你惹我生氣了。	You made me angry.
他極爲生氣。	He became stirred up.
她生氣極了。	She was in a savage mood.
她愛生氣。	She is swift to anger.
他容易生氣。	He is easily offended. 回 He is quick at taking offence. He is liable to get angry. He angers easily. He was prone to anger.
我假裝生氣。	I sham angry.
別惹我生氣。	Do not draw my anger down. 回 Don´t provoke me to anger.

你爲何生氣?	Why do you feel offended?
什麼使你生氣?	What makes you angry?
你這麼生氣是爲什麼?	What are you so mad at?
你生氣了嗎?	Are you angry?
你還生氣嗎?	Have you pulled out of anger?
生氣了嗎?	Got the grumps?
誰惹你生氣了?	Who occasioned your anger?
沒有生氣的緣由。	There is no occasion to be angry.
不要生氣。	Don´t be angry. 回 Don´t get angry. You keep your hair on.
他莫名地生氣。	He was unaccountably irritated.
我無意令她生氣。	I do not mean to drive her mad.
他們實在叫我生氣!	They really get across me!
我知道他爲什麼生氣。	I know why he was in temper.
我很怕她生氣。	I was fearful of her anger.
我不想跟你説話。	I don´t want to talk to you.
別管我!	Leave me alone!
他無緣無故就發怒。	He angers with little or no provocation.

爲難 Embarrassed

他使我爲難。	He is putting me on the spot.
你使我非常爲難。	You place me in a very difficult position.
真爲難!	How embarrassing!
我覺得很爲難。	I was very embarrassed.
一定讓你很爲難吧。	It must have been very embarrassing.
他一點也没讓我爲難。	He did not embarrass me in the slightest.
你顯得好像很爲難的樣子。	You look very confused.
這件事真叫人有點爲難啊。	This is somewhat embarrassing.
他爲難得臉都紅了。	He was so embarrassed that his face turned red.
我爲難得把目光轉到別處去了。	I looked away in embarrassment.
他的問題令你很尷尬。	You were embarrassed at his question.
我爲難得要死。	I could have died away with embarrassment.
我看他們并不是有意使你爲難。	I think they didn´t mean to be hard on you.
對我來說是多麼爲難啊。	It was a struggle for me.
這是件爲難的事。	This is an awkward matter.

害 羞 Shy

別害羞!	Don´t be shy!
你幹什麼都害羞。	You are shy in doing anything.
他是個害羞的男孩。	He is a shy boy.
我很容易害羞。	I blushed by miles.
他在陌生人面前害羞。	He is shy in front of strangers.
我有點害羞。	I am rather bashful. 回 I´m a little shy.
你有些害羞。	You are kind of shy.
我忘記了害羞。	I forgot my shyness.
她害羞，說話輕聲細語的。	She is a shy soft-spoken person.
你不必對此感到害羞。	You don´t need to be shy of it.
害羞使她說話結結巴巴。	Shyness made her speak in a halting manner.
她太害羞，沒有向他打招呼。	She was too shy to notice him.
無論她到哪裏，她都顯得害羞。	Wherever she went, she appeared bashful.
我是個極端害羞的小孩。	I am an extremely shy child.
他給我的第一印象是害羞。	My first impression on him is that he is shy.

難 過 Sad

聽到這事我很難過。	I am sorry to hear that.
聽到那消息我很難過。	I was upset over hearing the news.
我爲他感到難過。	I am sorry for him. 注解 爲了强調程度我們還會這樣說：I do feel sorry for him. 我真爲他難過。I feel sorry for him deeply. 我深深爲他感到難過。
你看起來很難過。	You look upset.
你難過嗎？	Are you feeling sad?
我覺得很難過。	I feel very bad. 同 I feel very sad.
我心情不好。	I feel depressed.
你爲什麼難過？	Why are you feeling so down?
我怎麼不難過？	How could I not be sad?
時至今日，回想起來，我仍然難過。	Even now the thought of it agonizes me.
我見她在哭，感到難過極了。	It breaks my heart to see her crying.
不要爲那事太難過了。	Don´t get yourself in such a stew about it.
我對這個意外感到很難過。	I feel bad about the accident.

Conversation
【交　　談】

- 同　意
- 反　對
- 拒　絕
- 請　求
- 商　量
- 責　備
- 道　歉
- 道　謝
- 抱　怨

同 意 Agree

好啊!	**Sounds good to me.** A: Let's go to Chinatown for lunch. (我們去中國城吃午餐。) B: Sounds good to me. (好啊!)
我認爲這個問題很重要。	**I think it´s very important.** A: What do you think of it? (你怎麽想的?) B: I think it's very important. (我認爲這個問題很重要。)
在這點上我同意你的觀點。	**I agree with that.** A: I find her very aloof and unfriendly. (我覺得她非常冷淡,不好相處。) B: I agree with that. (在這點上我同意你的觀點。)
我支持你。	**I´m with you.** A: I just want to quit and do something else. (我想辭職去做其他的工作。) B: I'm with you. (我支持你。)
我完全贊同。	**I´m all for it.** A: How does the plan strike you? (你覺得這個計劃怎麽樣?) B: This is a very good plan, I'm all for it. (這是個好計劃,我完全贊同。) 
我也這麽認爲。	**I think so, too.** A: Everything in Tokyo are too expensive. (東京的物價太貴。) B: I think so, too. (我也這樣認爲。)
一切聽你的。	**Anything you say!** A: Let's see a movie. (我們去看電影吧。) B: Anything you say! (一切聽你的。)

你說了算。

You´re in charge.

A: Let's go to have some drinks. (我們去喝點東西吧。)
B: You're in charge. (你說了算。)

聽你的。

You´re the boss.

A: How about go to the movie theater after we finish our work? (完成我們手頭的工作後去看電影,怎麼樣?)
B: You're the boss. (聽你的。)

没有异議。

No objection!

A: Is that arrangement ok?
(這樣的安排可以嗎?)
B: No objection! (没有异議!)

注解 objection "异議"、"反對"、"不服從"、"反對理由"。

我不反對。

I don´t have any objection to it.

A: What do you think of my proposal?
(你覺得我的建議怎麼樣?)
B: I don't have any objection to it. (我不反對。)

我沒問題。

No problem here.

A: How's tomorrow? (明天怎麼樣?)
B: No problem here. (你說了算。)

我沒意見。

Sounds alright to me.

這對我來說很好。

That´s fine with me.
同 **That sounds like a good idea to me.**

聽起來不錯。

That sounds good!

A: How about going to the zoo? (去動物園怎麼樣?)
B: That sounds good! (聽起來不錯。)

很好呀!

Fine. 同 **good.**

A: How's everything? (一切都好嗎?)
B: Fine. (很好呀!)

注解 "Fine", "good", 這是種常用的表達方式,表示帶有"無可挑剔的"、"不錯的"、"好的"等語感。

這個可以接受。	**It´s acceptable.**
那就行了。	**That´s fair.** A: How does that sound? (那樣行嗎？) B: That's fair. (那就行了。) 注解 That's fair. 用于聽到對方給予妥協性的回答時，就對方的意見或行爲作出答復，含有"這樣才公平、公正"的語氣。
你說的真對 (我也有同樣的感覺)。	**You can say that again.** A: That meeting was awful. (那個會開得真糟糕。) B: You can say that again. (我也有同樣感覺。) 注解 You can say that again.表示"我的看法和你完全一致"，帶有同情的語感。
我也那樣認爲。	**I´ll say.**
確實！	**Definitely.**
好像挺有意思。	**Sounds like fun.** A: Let's go out! (我們出去玩吧！) B: Sounds like fun. (那一定很有意思。)
當然，一定！	**You bet!**
的確如此！	**That is for sure.**
我敢打賭。	**I´d bet on it.**
毫無疑問。	**It goes without saying.**
真是太棒了。	**That is great!**
好主意。	**Good idea.**
你說的有一部分是對的。	**What you say is partly right.** 同 **You are partially correct.**
我部分同意。	**I agree with you partially.**

反 對 Object

我不能同意。	**I can´t agree.** 注解 I can't agree.“我不能同意你的意見”,比較禮貌的說法。
我反對。	**I don´t agree.** 注解 I don't agree. 比 I can't agree. 的語氣還要强烈,給人一種直接反對的印象。
我認爲我是正確的。	**I know I´m correct.**
恐怕我不能贊同你。	**I´m afraid I can´t agree with you.** A: All politicians are liars. (所有的政治家都是騙子。) B: I'm afraid I can't agree with you. (恐怕我不能贊同你。)
我懷疑。	**I doubt it.** A: Do you think it's true? (你覺得那是真的嗎?) B: I doubt it. (我很懷疑。)
我不這麼認爲。	**I don´t think so.**
才不會發生呢。	**It´s not likely to happen.**
反對!	**Objection!** A: We found out that he wasn't there. (我們發現他没有在那兒。) B: Objection! (反對!)
你不是這麼説的。	**That´s not what you said.** 同 **You didn´t say that.**
我無法相信。	**I can´t buy that!** A: I'm telling the truth. (我説的都是真的。) B: I can't buy that! (我無法相信。) 注解 buy 除了“買”以外,還有“相信”、“承認”的意思。

那太荒謬了。

That´s ridiculous!

我不敢相信。

I refuse to believe that.

餿主意。

Bad idea.

A: Let's cheat. (我們糊弄一回吧。)
B: Bad idea. (餿主意。)

注解 Bad idea. 用于不同意對方的提議時。

那可不好哦!

No good.

A: How is it? (怎麼樣?)
B: No good. (那可不好哦!)

注解 No good. 用于否定對方的意圖、打算、計劃時。是"那樣不好"、"不行"的意思。這種表達方式讓人覺得說話人有與對方不同的主意。

算了吧!

Let´s not.

A: Let's go drinking. (我們去喝酒吧!)
B: Let's not. (算了吧!)

注解 Let's not. 否定、拒絕對方的提議、定義、暗示。

那怎麼可能。

That´s impossible. 同 **That can´t be.**

A: He's guilty. (他有罪。)
B: That's impossible. (那怎麼可能。)

那完全是胡說八道。

That´s absolute nonsense.

A: I saw you steal the money. (我看見你偷人家錢了。)
B: That's absolute nonsense. (那完全是胡說八道。)

別那麼不講道理。

Don´t be so unreasonable.

那根本不可能。

That´s out of the question.

行不通。

It won´t work.

A: I think it's a good idea. (我覺得那是一個好主意。)
B: It won't work. (恐怕行不通。)

注解 It won't work. 意爲 "好像怎麼也不行"、"好像不順利"、"好像不妥當",是 No good. 的較正式的表達方式。

不經常這樣。	**Not always.** A: You always work late. (你總是工作到很晚啊。) B: Not always. (不經常這樣。)
不太想。	**Not really.** A: Do you want to go out for dinner? (你想不想去外面吃晚飯？) B: Not really. (不太想。)  注解 Not really. 不能同意對方的意見或信息時，有禮貌地加以否定。
對這一點我難相信。	**I find that hard to swallow.**
恐怕我們在這一點上達不成共識。	**I´m afraid we don´t see eye to eye on this.** 注解 see eye to eye on something. "對某事看法一致。"貌的説法。
我覺得還是眼見爲實。	**I´ll believe it when I see it.**
不，我不會同意的。別跟我這兒費口舌。	**No, I won´t agree! Don´t waste your breath.**
你錯的太離譜了。	**You´re way off base.** 注解 off base "棒球不在壘上"此處指"與事實不符"，way 是副詞，意思是"非常，大大地"。
你太言過其實了。	**You´re really stretching the truth.** 注解 stretch "濫用，誇大"。
我要和你好好談談你在會上説的那些話。	**I must take issue with you over what you said at the meeting.** 注解 take issue with someone "對某人的觀點提出异議。"
恐怕我的看法和你不一樣。	**I´m afraid I have a different opinion.**
我明白你的觀點，但我的確不能贊同。	**I see your point, but I can´t really agree with you.**

拒 絕 Reject

我希望可以，但是我得去見一個朋友。

I wish I could, but I have to meet my friend.

A: Could you work overtime tonight?
(今天晚上能加個班嗎？)
B: I wish I could, but I have to meet my friend.
(我希望可以，但是我得去見一個朋友。)

我挺想去的，但是沒有時間。

I´d love to, but I don´t have time.

A: What about go shopping this afternoon?
(下午去逛街怎麼樣？)
B: I'd love to, but I don't have time.
(我挺想去的，但是沒有時間。)

我不願意。

I won´t.

注解 I wish I could, but...委婉地拒絕對方要求的表達方式。

不，謝謝。

No, thank you.

A: Do you need help? (要我來幫你嗎？)
B: No, thank you. (不，謝謝。)

注解 No, thank you. 雖然很感激，但必須拒絕時使用。

我真的不要。

I really don´t want it.

A: Take one. (拿一個吧。)
B: I really don't want it. (我真的不要。)

真抱歉，我不能幫助你。

I´m sorry I can´t help you.
同 **I´m sorry I can´t be any help.**

A: Where is the London Hotel? (請問倫敦飯店在哪兒？)
B: I'm sorry I can't help you. (對不起，我幫不了你。)

我很樂意，可我幫不了你。

I wish I could help you, but I can´t.

A: Could you help me get a job? (您能幫我找一份工作嗎?)
B: I wish I could help you, but I can't.
(我很樂意，可惜我幫不了你。)

這事我什麼辦法也沒有。	**I can´t do anything about it.** **回 There is nothing I can do about it.** A: You have to help me. (你得幫幫我。) B: I can't do anything about it. (這事我什麼辦法也沒有。)
我無法滿足你的願望。	**I can´t make that happen.** A: I want to work for this company. (我想在這家公司工作。) B: Sorry, I can't make that happen. (對不起，我無法滿足你的願望。)
我沒那份心情。	**I´m not in the mood.** **回 I don´t feel like it.** A: Do you want to dance? (想跳舞嗎？) B: I'm not in the mood. (我沒那份心情。)
很遺憾，我現在有件急事。	**I´m afraid I´ve got urgent business now.** A: I'm afraid I've got urgent business now. (很遺憾，我現在有件急事。) B: That's a shame. (真是太遺憾了。)
我有別的事。	**I have other business to take care of.** A: Are you free today? (你今天有時間嗎？) B: No, I have other business to take care of. (沒有，我有別的事。)
對不起，我現在正忙着呢。	**I´m sorry, but I´m busy right now.** A: Can you help me fix my bicycle? (你能幫我修理自行車嗎？) B: I'm sorry, but I'm busy right now. (對不起，我現在正忙着呢。)
對不起，我有急事。	**I´m sorry, but I´m in a hurry.** A: Come over for dinner tonight. (今晚過來吃晚餐吧！) B: I'm sorry, but I'm in a hurry. (對不起，我有急事。)
我就算了吧。	**Count me out.** 注解 Count me out. 意爲不要算上我。在自己不願意參加或不願意加入時使用。相反，Count me in 的意思是算上我。

我寧可不要（我不想這麼做）。	**I´d rather not.** A: Let's go drinking. (我們去喝酒吧。) B: I'd rather not. (我還是不去了吧。)
已經足夠了。	**I´ve had enough.** A: How about more salad? (再來點兒沙拉，怎麼樣?) B: No, thank you. I've had enough. (不，謝謝，已經足够了。) 注解 Enough 表示"所有量，接受量足够了"。也可以用來表示有够多的麻煩和痛苦時。
很遺憾，今天我不太方便。	**Unfortunately, it´s not convenient for me today.** A: Why don't we have dinner together? (我們去吃晚飯吧。) B: Unfortunately, it's not convenient for me today. (很遺憾，今天我不太方便。)
没說到點兒上。	**That´s beside the point.** A: If it hadn't rained, I would have done it. (要是没下雨的話，我就可以做，可是……) B: That's beside the point. (根本没說到點兒上。) 注解 beside the point 表示"估計錯的"、"没抓住中心的"。
不行!	**Not on your life!** A: Would you lie for me? (你能幫我撒個謊嗎？) B: Not on your life! (不行！) 注解 Not on your life! 表示强烈的拒絕。

絶對不可以。	**Certainly not.** A: Can we do it like this? (我們能這麼做嗎？) B: Certainly not. (絶對不可以。)
機會渺茫!	**A fat chance!** A: Do you think he will win? (你覺得他會贏嗎？) B: A fat chance! (機會很渺茫！)
不管什么理由，不行就是不行。	**Not for any reason!** A: It was an accident. Could you give me one more chance? (這是一場意外，能給我多一次機會嗎？) B: Not for any reason! (不管什麼理由，不行就是不行！)

沒門！	**No way!** A: Can you just help me do it? (你能幫我做這件事嗎？) B: No way! (沒門！)
沒戲！	**Not a chance!** A: What about invite him to dinner. (不如請他吃飯吧！) B: Not a chance! He's so hard to please. (沒戲！他這人很難取悅。) 注解 Not a chance in the world! 表示更爲强烈的拒絕。絶不允許！
絶不允許！	**Over my dead body!** A: Would you loan me $100,000? (你能借給我 10 萬美元嗎?) B: Over my dead body! (絶不可能！) 注解 Over my dead body! 表示"衹要我還未閉眼，絶不讓……"、"完全不可能"。
很遺憾，恐怕不行。	**I´m afraid not.** A: Is this the smoking section? (這兒是吸烟區嗎？) B: No, I'm afraid not. (很遺憾，好像不是。) 注解 I'm afraid not. 用于雖然對方也許不想聽，或者不相信，但不得不説 No(不)時。這是一種委婉的否定表達方式，含有表示同情對方的心情。
除了這個，其他的都行！	**Everything but this.** A: Let's go bungee jumping. (我們去蹦極吧！) B: Everything but this. (除了這個，其他的都行！)
你以爲我會答應嗎？	**Do you expect me to accept that?** A: Can you help me cheat on tomorrow's English test? (明天的英語考試你能幫我作弊嗎？) B: That's just too much to ask. Do you expect me to accept that? (這個要求太過分了，你以爲我會答應嗎？)
我想是不可以的。	**I would suppose not.**
我不想這樣。	**I´d rather not.** A: Suppose we will wait till this evening. (假如我們要等到晚上。) B: I'd rather not. (我不想這樣。)

請　求 Request

我可以請您幫個忙嗎?

Do you mind if I ask you a favor?

A: Do you mind if I ask you a favor?
(我可以請您幫個忙嗎?)
B: No, not at all. (沒問題,完全可以。)

能幫幫我嗎?

Would you give me a hand?
同 **Would you please help me?**
Would you mind giving me a hand?
Could you help me out?

對不起……

I´m sorry to bother you……

A: I'm sorry to bother you, but can you help me?
(對不起,能幫我一下嗎?)
B: No problem. (沒問題。)

我能用一下你的車嗎?

Could I possibly use your car?

A: Could I possibly use your car? (我能用一下你的車嗎?)
B: Of course. (當然可以。)

注解 Could I possibly...? 的意思是"我可不可以…… / 可不可以讓我……"

您能爲我做這個嗎?

Would you please do this for me?

能把聲音關小聲點嗎?

Would you please turn it down?

A: Would you please turn it down? (能把聲音關小點嗎?)
B: All right! (好吧!)

注解 turn down 是"關小"電視、收音機等的聲音。
另外關于 turn 還有以下幾種用法:
turn up (開大電視、收音機等的聲音)
turn off (關上電視、收音機等)
turn on (打開電視、收音機等)

我想求你件事行嗎?

Can I ask you a favor?

我想打聽點兒事。

May I ask you something?

A: May I ask you something? (我想打聽點兒事。)
B: Sure. Go ahead. (當然,請說吧。)

您能開車送我到那家店嗎?

Would you drive me to the store?

A: Would you drive me to the store?
(您能開車送我到那家店嗎?)
B: My pleasure. (可以啊!)

你今天晚上如果能給我打個電話的話，我將非常感激。

I´d appreciate it if you could call me tonight.

A: I'd appreciate it if you could call me tonight.
(你今天晚上如果能給我打個電話的話,我將非常感激。)
B: I'd be glad to. (我非常願意。)

別這樣，我知道你可以做到的!

Come on, I know you can do it!

A: Sorry, I can't help you. (對不起,我幫不了你!)
B: Come on, I know you can do it!
(別這樣,我知道你可以做到的。)

請幫我把行李拿上來吧。

Have my luggage take up, please.

A: Have my luggage take up, please.
(請幫我把行李拿上來吧!)
B: Wow! It's really heavy.
(哇! 這行李真夠重的。)

求求你了!

Please! Please!

A: Help me once more. Plesse! Please!
(再幫我一次吧! 求求你了!)
B: Ok, it is the last time. (好吧,最後一次了。)

我做不好，請幫幫我。

I can´t do it well. Please help me.

A: I can't do it well. Please help me. (我做不好,請幫幫我。)
B: You must do it by yourself this time.
(這次你要自己做。)

全拜托了,邁克。

Thanks for what you´ll do, Mike.

A: Thanks for what you'll do, Mike. (全拜托了,邁克。)
B: I will try my best. (我會盡力的。)

拜托了,安娜,拜托。我需要你幫我。

Please, Anna. Please. I need your help.

A: Please, Anna. Please. I need your help.
(拜托了,安娜,拜托。我需要你幫我。)
B: Give me some time to think it over. (給我時間考慮一下。)

上次我幫了你,這次換你幫我了。

I help you last time, it is your turn this time.

A: Sorry, I am very busy.
(對不起,我很忙。)
B: I help you last time, it is your turn this time.
(上次我幫了你,這次換你幫我了。)

我全靠你了。

I´m counting on you.

A: I'm counting on you. (我全靠你了!)
B: I won't let you down. (我不會讓你失望的。)

你是我唯一的希望。

You´re my only hope.

A: You're my only hope. (你是我唯一的希望。)
B: Don't expect too much from me. (别對我期望太高了。)

能請你幫我搬一下這個箱子嗎?

Would you please move the box for me?

請幫我復印一下這封信。

Please copy this letter for me.

能幫我換點錢嗎?

Could I have some change?

A: Could I have some change? (能幫我換點錢嗎?)
B: Sorry, I don't have any change on me.
(對不起,我身上没有零錢了。)

請幫我把我的信傳給她好嗎?

Would you deliver my letter to her?

你能幫我補一補這件衣服嗎?

Can you mend the coat for me?

幫我把窗户打開。

Open the window, please!

商　量 Discuss

我有事必須告訴你。	**I need to tell you something.** A: I need to tell you something. (我有事必須告訴你。) B: What's wrong? (怎麼啦？)
我會把一切都告訴你！	**I'll fill you in.** A: Did you hear that sound last night? What happened? (你昨晚聽到那個聲音了嗎？發生什麼事了？) B: Ok, I'll fill you in. (好，我把一切告訴你。)
這是一個秘密。	**It´s a secret.** A: It's a secret. (這是一個秘密。) B: I won't say a word. (我一個字都不說出去。)
我知道的大概就是這些。	**That is about all I know.** A: What else do you know? (其他你還知道些什麼？) B: That is about all I know. (我知道的大概就是這些。)
我就直說吧。	**I'll level with you.** A: Quit lying to me! (不要對我說謊話。) B: All right. I'll level with you. (好吧，我就直說吧。) 注解 level 表示"把……弄平"，但在這兒表示"說話不拐彎，直說"。
我們接下來怎麼做？	**Where do we go from here?** A: I think most of the preperation has been done. (我想我們大部分的準備工作都已經完成了。) B: Where do we go from here? (我們接下來怎麼做？)
洗耳恭聽。	**I am all your ears.** A: Hey, Mary, I have something important to tell you. (瑪麗，我有些很重要的事情要跟你說。) B: I am all your ears. (洗耳恭聽。)

和你說實話。	**Give this to you straight.** A: Please tell me the truth. (麻煩你，直接告訴我是怎麼回事吧。) B: I truly want to give this to you straight, but this is not the right time. (我真的很想和你說實話，可現在時機未到。)
我們私下裏說。	**This is just between you and me.**
別拐彎抹角了。	**Don´t beat around the bush.** A: In my way of thinking, it's not the best solution. (就我看來，這不是最佳的解決方案。) B: Don't beat around the bush. (別拐彎抹角了。)
我告訴你真相。	**I´ll tell you the truth.** A: Is that so? (真的是那樣嗎？) B: Ok, I'll tell you the truth. (好吧，我告訴你真相。)
說下去。	**Keep talking.** A: I am in hot water. (我遇到麻煩了。) B: Keep talking. (說下去。) 注解 in hot water 是"有麻煩；陷于困境"的意思。
我這麼說好了。	**Let me put it this way.** A: What's this all about? (這是怎麼回事？) B: Let me put it this way. (我這麼說好了。)
你最好三思而後行。	**You´d better look before you leap.** A: I am not kidding. (我不是跟你開玩笑的。) B: You'd better look before you leap. (你最好三思而後行。)
看情況再說。	**That depends.**
此話當真？	**Do you really mean it?**
我完全可以肯定。	**I couldn´t be more sure.**
一看就知道！	**That figures.**

慢慢來,不着急。	Take your time.
面對現實吧!	Let´s face it.
原來如此。	So that explains.
你到底想讓我怎麼做?	What do you want me to do?
我說得夠清楚嗎?	Do I make myself clear?
沒有退路了。	There is no turning back.
你想怎麼處理?	How would you handle it?
你的看法如何?	What do you make of this?
這對你有什麼好處?	What´s in it for you?
你覺得如何?	What do you say?
由你決定。	It´s up to you.
今天就到這裏吧。	Let´s call it a day.
出事了。	Something´s come up.
記住那件事!	Keep that in mind.
尚未確定。	It´s up in the air.
我會留意的。	I will keep my eyes open.
我們再看看。	We´ll see.
我明白了。	I got it.
答案就在那裏。	The answer is out there.

責 備 Blame

都是你的錯！	**It´s all your fault!** A: It's all your fault! (都是你的錯！) B: I'm not really in control of that. (這不是我能控制的。)
這是你的過錯。	**You´re to blame.** A: You're to blame. (這是你的過錯。) B: Why me? (怎麼是我？)
你站在我的立場上想想。	**Put yourself in my shoes.** 同 **Try to see it from my point of view.** **Try to see it my way.** A: We will not take your illness into consideration. (我們沒考慮到你生病。) B: Put yourself in my shoes. (你們該爲我想想。)
你就不覺得害臊嗎?	**Aren´t you ashamed of yourself?**  A: I did what I thought was right. (我衹是做我認爲對的事情。) B: Aren't you ashamed of yourself? (難道你就不覺得害臊嗎？) 注解 ashamed"做了不好的事感到的羞愧和慚愧"。 be ashamed of... 表示"……覺得害臊"。
你就不能嚴肅點嗎?	**Can you be serious for once?** A: I don't see what the big deal is. (我想不通這有什麼大不了的。) B: Can you be serious for once? (你就不能嚴肅點嗎？)
你這麼說什麼意思?	**What do you mean by saying so?** A: Don't you make any mistakes? (你就沒有犯錯嗎？) B: What do you mean by saying so? (你說這話什麼意思?)
你爲什麼老挑我的刺兒?	**Why are you picking on me?**

別拿我開心了。	**Don´t pull my leg.** A: Isn't that good? (這樣不是挺好的嗎？) B: Don't pull my leg. (別拿我開心了。)
我早說過了吧。	**I told you so.** A: I got in trouble for lying. (因爲撒謊，我闖禍了。) B: I told you so. You shouldn't lie. (我早說過吧，你不該撒謊。)
這可全爲了你！	**It´s for your own good!** A: I don't want to. (我不想做。) B: It's for your own good! (這可全爲了你！)
別裝傻！	**Don´t play dumb!** A: I don't know. (我不知道。) B: Don't play dumb! (別裝傻！) 注解 dumb 除了"啞巴"之外還有"愚笨的"意思，所以 play dumb 意爲"裝傻"。 
別幹那種傻事！	**Don´t act stupid.** A: Don't act stupid! (別幹那種傻事！) B: It's just a joke. (衹是個玩笑。)
你幹嗎要幹那種事？	**Why are you doing that?** A: Why are you doing that? (你幹嗎要幹那種事？) B: Why not? (爲什麼不能幹？)
我已經聽够了你那些無聊話了。	**I´ve had enough of your nonsense.** A: Why don't you believe me? (爲什麼你不相信我呢？) B: I've had enough of your nonsense. (我已經聽够了你那些無聊話。) 注解 nonsense"没有意義的話，戲言，荒唐的想法"。
下次能不能禮貌點兒？	**Could you be more polite next time?**
你知道你自己在幹些什麼嗎？	**What do you think you´re doing?**
你在騙我吧？	**You tricked me.**

我不明白你爲什麼不早告訴我。	I wonder why you couldn´t have told me earlier.
別把我拉進去。	Don´t involve me.
你應該更小心一點的。	You should be more careful.
你應爲你自己感到羞恥。	You ought to be ashamed of yourself.
你真是一點用都沒有。	You are really good for nothing.
你做這件事情是多麼的荒唐。	How absurd you to do that.
你瘋了!	You´re out of your mind!
怎會做這種事!	What a thing to do!
我不想再聽你說的謊話。	I don´t want to hear any more of your lies.
別胡說八道。	Don´t be ridiculous! 同 Don´t be silly! Don´t talk silly. Don´t say stupid things.
我對你忍無可忍了。	I´m out of patience with you.
你怎麼能做這麼愚蠢的事情?	How can you do such a foolish thing?
你太淘氣了。	You are too naughty.
你本來至少可以避免這樣做。	You might at least have avoided doing that.
你騙人的把戲可蒙不了我。	None of your tricks will work on me.

道 歉 Apologize

請原諒。	Excuse me.
很抱歉。	I´m so sorry.
非常抱歉。	I´m awfully sorry.
爲此我非常抱歉。	I´m terribly sorry about that.
我道歉。	I apologize.
請原諒我。	Please forgive me.
希望你能原諒我。	I hope you will excuse me.
好像我該向你道個歉。	It seems I owe you an apology.
我誠心誠意向你道歉。	You have my sincere apology.
請接受我誠心誠意的道歉。	Please accept my sincere apology.
我真的是很抱歉。	I can´t tell you how sorry I am.
你不知道我感到多麼抱歉。	You cannot believe how sorry I am.
語言無法描述我對你的歉意。	Words cannot describe how sorry I am.
我真不知該說什麼好。	I just don´t know what to say.
我真的感到很內疚。	I really feel bad about it.

不好意思打擾你。	Sorry to be a bother.
不好意思打擾你。	Sorry to be a pest.
抱歉，又來打擾你。	Sorry to disturb you again.
對不起，真不想打擾你。	I´m sorry, I didn´t mean to bother you.
恐怕我給你帶來了不少麻煩。	I´m afraid I´ve brought you a lot of trouble.
給你造成諸多不便，我很抱歉。	I´m sorry to have caused you so much inconvenience.
對不起添麻煩了。	Sorry about the inconvenience.
我兒子一定給你帶來不少麻煩。	My son must have put you to a lot of trouble.
我爲我的所作所爲向你道歉。	I´m sorry for what I´ve done.
我不該那麼做。	I shouldn´t have done that.
我應該先徵得你的同意。	I should have asked you first.
我的確不是故意的。	I honestly didn´t mean it.
我并不想要那麼做。	I didn´t mean to do that.
事情鬧成那樣并非我的本意。	I didn´t mean it that way.
我不知道怎麼會發生那樣的事。	I don´t know how that could have happened.
你是對的，我錯了。我道歉。	You were right and I was wrong. I apologize.

是我的錯，我真的感到很難過。	It´s my fault. I really feel bad about it.
這事兒全怪我，我會盡力補救。	It´s all my fault. I´ll try to make it up to you.
是我的錯，不會再發生類似的事情了。	My mistake. It won´t happen again.
非常抱歉，我當時真糊塗。	It was so stupid of me. I really do apologize.
對不起，我說錯話了。	I´m sorry, I spoke out of turn. 注解 out of turn 輕率，不合時宜。
我應該爲昨天晚上的事向你道歉。	I owe you an apology for what I did last night.
請原諒，我不是有意惹你生氣。	Forgive me, I didn´t mean to offend you.
因爲我的失誤給你添麻煩了，請接受我的道歉。	Please accept my apologies for any trouble my mistake has caused you.
關于你的損失，請接受我真心道歉。	Please accept my sincere apology for your loss.
我爲我的無禮真誠地道歉。	I sincerely apologize for my rudeness.
請接受我的道歉，也謝謝你們大家的關心。	Please accept my apology, and thank you for your concern.
我希望大家都能够接受我的道歉并給我一次機會。	I hope you all accept my apology and give me a chance.
我爲我的錯誤道歉。	I apologize for my mistake.
我真誠地表示道歉！	I express the apology sincerely!
我爲所發生的事情道歉。	I apologize for what happened.

道 謝 Thank

謝謝！

Thank you!

Thanks!

A: Thank you! (謝謝！)
B: Not at all. (不用謝！)

真是太謝謝你了。

Thank you very much.

A: Thank you very much. (真是太謝謝你了。)
B: You are welcome. (不用客氣。)

真的很感謝你。

I really appreciate it.

A: Here's a present for your birthday.
(這是給你的生日禮物。)
B: How nice! I really appreciate it.
(好漂亮，真的很感謝你。)

我真不知道該怎麼感謝你。

I don´t know how I can possibly thank you enough.

A: I don't know how I can possibly thank you enough.
(我真不知道該怎麼感謝你。)
B: Don't mention it. (不必謝。)

你的幫助讓我倍受感激。

Your help was greatly appreciated.

A: I'll have everything prepared for you when you get here. (你來時我會爲你準備好一切的。)
B: Your help was greatly appreciated.
(你的幫助讓我倍受感激。)

感謝您爲我們所做的一切。

Thank you for everything.

A: Thank you for everything.
(感謝您爲我們所做的一切。)
B: It's all right. Everyone would have done the same in my position. (這沒什麼，任何人在這種情況下都會這麼做的。)

我要表達我的誠摯的謝意。	**I´d like to express my gratitude.** A: I'd like to express my gratitude. (我要表達我的誠摯的謝意。) B: I'm delighted I was able to help. (能幫助你,我很高興。)
多虧有你，我們才能準時完成。	**Thanks to you, we made it on time.** A: Thanks to you, we made it on time. (多虧有你,我們才能準時完成。) B: It was the least I could do. (我祇不過是盡力而已。)
你真是大好人。	**You´re one in a million.** A: I fixed your computer and you can use it now. (電腦我幫你恢復好了,你可以用了。) B: You're one in a million. (你真是個大好人。)
你最棒了。	**You´re the greatest.** A: You're the greatest. (你最棒了。) B: Thanks. I'm flattered. (謝謝,你過獎了。) 注解 flattered 的意思是：高興的, 感到榮幸的;過分誇贊高興的。
若是沒有你，我不可能做到。	**I couldn´t do it without you.** A: I couldn't do it without you. (若是沒有你,我不可能做到。) B: It is my pleasure. (我很樂意幫忙。) 
我非常感激你的幫助。	**I´m truly grateful for your help.** A: I'm truly grateful for your help. (我非常感激你的幫助。) B: It's my pleasure. (能幫到你我很高興。)
真是太感謝你幫我把信給翻譯了。	**It was so nice of you to translate the letter for me.** A: It was so nice of you to translate the letter for me. (真是太感謝你幫我把信給翻譯了。) B: I also learn something from it. (我也從中學了些東西。)
您幫了我大忙。	**You´ve done me a great favor.** A: I've had your car fixed. (我已經叫人把車修好了。) B: You've done me a great favor. (您幫了我大忙。)

謝謝，您太好了。	**Thank you. It was very kind of you.** A: Thank you. It was very kind of you. (謝謝，您太好了。) B: There is nothing to thank me for. (沒有什麼可謝我的。)
要不是您的幫助，我真不知道該怎麼辦。	**I don´t know what I should have done without your help.** A: I don't know what I should have done without your help. (要不是您的幫助，我真不知道該怎麼辦。) B: It was a real pleasure for me to do it. (我很樂意這樣做。)
非常感謝你的邀請。	**Thank you very much for your invitation.** A: Do you enjoy your stay here? (你們玩得好嗎？) B: It's wonderful! Thank you very much for your invitation. (好極了！非常感謝你的邀請。)
您給我帶路真是太感謝了。	**It´s very good of you to show me the way.** A: It's very good of you to show me the way. (您給我帶路真是太感謝了。) B: Please don't mention it. (請不用客氣。)
我對你真是感激不盡。	**I really can´t thank you enough.** A: I really can't thank you enough. (我對你直是感激不盡。) B: I'm glad to serve you. (很高興能爲您效勞。)
非常感謝你能陪我來。	**I really appreciate you accompanying me here.** A: How is you interview? (你的面試怎麼樣？) B: Just fine, and I really appreciate you accompanying me here. (挺好的，非常感謝你能陪我來。)
真太感謝您幫我借了這些書。	**It´s so sweet of you to borrow those books for me.** A: It's so sweet of you to borrow those books for me. (真太感謝您幫我借了這些書。) B: It's just so convenient to do it. (這很方便的。)
首先，我要感謝您對我的友愛和問候。	**At the outset, I want to thank you for your kindness to me and for your compliments.**

抱 怨 Complain

太過分了。	This is too much.
真叫人忍無可忍。	That´s really the limit.
我再也受不了。	This is more than I can bear.
簡直想要了我的命。	I needed that like a hole in the head.
我已經受够了。	I´ve had enough of that!
恐怕我要提點意見。	I´m afraid I have a complaint to make.
你非得那麼做嗎?	Do you have to act like that?
你能不能別那麼做?	Would you mind not doing it?
這麼晚了。你能不能盡量保持安靜。	Would you please try to keep quiet at this hour?
我期待的可不是這樣的。	It´s not what I hoped for.
太不讓人滿意了。	That leaves a lot to be desired.
這離我想要的差遠了。	It´s a far cry from what I expected.
當時說好的可不是這個樣子。	I am not getting what I bargained for.
我被騙了。	I got a bum deal.
太亂了!	What a mess!

我這輩子沒見過這麼亂的地方。	Never in my life have I seen such a mess!
你真讓我慚愧!	You make me sick!
你真不應該那樣做。	You shouldn´t have done that!
別那樣和我說話!	Don´t talk to me like that!
別自以爲是。	Get over yourself.
真讓我失望。	I'm very disappointed.
我怎麼那麼倒霉。	What a black day!
別抱怨了。	Stop complaining.
別訴苦了。	Quit whining.
我說你別再訴苦了。	For heaven´s sake stop whining.
別總這麼愛抱怨。	Don´t be so grumpy.
不要總是牢騷滿腹。	Don´t be such a grouch.
別老是哼哼唧唧的。	Don´t be such a moaner.
我希望你別老這麼煩我。	I wish you´d stop nagging me.
我不明白你爲什麼要這樣小題大作。	I don´t see why you are kicking up such a fuss.
我知道你的感受,可是也沒必要這樣沒完沒了。	I know how you feel, but there´s no need to go on and on about it.
別再抱怨了，抱怨再多也無濟于事。	Stop complaining. There is nothing to help.

Appendix
【附　　錄】

- 美國節假日
- 諺　語
- 警告 / 提示

美國節假日
US Holidays and Festivals

1月1日 新　年	New Year´s Day
1月 *** 日 馬丁路德金生日 (1月的第三個星期一)	Martin Luther King Day
2月14日 情人節	Valentine´s Day
2月*** 日 總統日 (2月的第三個星期一)	Presidents´ Day
3月17日 聖帕特裏克節	St. Patrick´s Day
4月1日 愚人節	April Fools Day
4月 *** 日 復活節 (一般指春分月圓後第一個星期日)	Easter
5月 *** 日 母親節 (五月的第二個星期日)	Mother´s Day
5月 *** 日 國殤日 (五月的最後一個星期一)	Memorial Day
6月 *** 日 父親節 (六月的第三個星期日)	Father´s Day
7月4日 獨立日	Independence Day
9月 *** 日 勞工節 (九月的第一個星期一)	Labor Day
10月12日 哥倫布日	Columbus Day
10月31日 萬聖節	Halloween
11月11日 退伍軍人節	Veterans Day
11月 *** 日 感恩節 (十一月的最後一個星期四)	Thanksgiving Day
12月25日 聖誕節	Christmas

諺 語
Proverbs

不善始者不善終。	A bad beginning makes a bad ending.
一鳥在手勝過雙鳥在林。	A bird in the hand is worth than two in the bush.
愛挑的擔子不嫌重。	A burden of one´s choice is not felt.
行動勝于言辭。	Actions speak louder than words.
吃一塹,長一智。	A fall into a pit, a gain in your wit. 同 Experience must be bought.
患難見真情。	A friend in need is a friend indeed.
良好的開端是成功的一半。	A good beginning is half done.
好書如摯友。	A good book is a good friend.
美名勝過美貌。	A good fame is better than a good face.
說大話者多謊言。	A great talker is a great liar.
濃縮的都是精品。	A little body often harbors a great soul.
天下沒有不散的筵席。	All good things come to an end.
海納百川。	All rivers run into sea.
以眼還眼,以牙還牙。	An eye for an eye and a tooth for a tooth.
少壯不努力，老大徒傷悲。	A young idler, an old beggar.

種瓜得瓜，種豆得豆。	As a man sows, so he shall reap.
好事不出門，壞事傳千裏。	Bad news has wings.
聽宜敏捷，言宜緩行。	Be swift to hear, slow to speak.
亡羊補牢，爲時不晚。	Better late than never.
物以類聚，人以群分。	Birds of a feather flock together.
血濃于水。	Blood is thicker than water.
公事公辦。	Business is business.
耳濡目染，身教言傳。	Children are what the mothers are.
知足者常樂。	Content is better than riches.
循序漸進。	Creep before you walk.
習慣是後天養成的。	Custom is a second nature.
入鄉隨俗。	Do as the Romans do.
凡事不可半途而廢。	Do nothing by halves.
今日事，今日畢。	Don´t put off till tomorrow what should be done today.
不要班門弄斧。	Don´t try to teach your grandmother to suck eggs.
來也匆匆，去也匆匆。	Easy come, easy go.
有利必有弊。	Every advantage has its disadvantage.
誰都有得意的時候。	Every dog has his day.

人吃飯是爲了活着，但活着不是爲了吃飯。	Eat to live, but not live to eat.
蘿卜青菜，各有所愛。	Every man has his hobbyhorse.
人人都有弱點。	Every man has his weak side.
分秒必爭。	Every minute counts.
說一遍，不如做一遍。	Example is better than percept.
事實勝于雄辯。	Fact speak louder than words.
失敗是成功之母。	Failure is the mother of success.
眼不見，心不煩。	Far from eye, far from heart. 同 Out of sight, out of mind.
恐懼源于無知。	Fear always springs from ignorance.
隔墻有耳。	Fields have eyes, and woods have ears.
先來先到。	First come, first served.
機遇偏愛善斷之人。	Fortune favors those who use their judgement.
天才不过是勤奋而已。	Genius is nothing but labor and diligence.
自助者天助。	God helps those who help themselves.
健康是最大的財富。	Good health is over wealth.
偉大的抱負造就偉大的人物。	Great hopes make great man.
英雄所見略同。	Great minds think alike.

貴人多忘事。	Great wits have short memories.
心貪手長。	Greedy folks have long arms.
做賊心虛。	Guilty consciences make men cowards.
一見鐘情難維久。	Hasty love, soon cold.
健康勝過財富。	Health is better than wealth.
兼聽則明。	Hear all parties.
祇有死人才不犯錯誤。	He is lifeless that is faultless.
不善律己,焉能正人。	He is not fit to command others that cannot command himself.
自嘲者不會讓人見笑。	He is not laughed at that laughs at himself first.
大智若愚。	He knows most who speaks least.
誰笑到最後,誰笑得最好。	He laughs best who laughs last.
逆水行舟,不進則退。	He who does not advance loses ground.
想不犯錯誤,就一事無成。	He who makes no mistakes makes nothing.
收獲與風險并存。	He who risks nothing gains nothing.
抱最好的希望,做最壞的打算。	Hope for the best, but prepare for the worst.
歷史往往重演。	History repeats itself.
誠實乃上策。	Honesty is the best policy.
脚踏兩條船,必定落空。	If you run after two hares, you will catch neither.

殺鷄取卵。	If you sell the cow, you sell her milk too.
活到老,學到老。	It is never too old to learn.
天有不測風雲，人有旦夕禍福。	It is the unforeseen that always happens.
不雨則已,一雨傾盆。	It never rains but it pours.
無所不能便一無所精。	Jack of all trades and master of none.
一箭雙雕。	Kill two birds with one stone.
知識就是力量。	Knowledge is power.
博學使人謙遜，無知使人驕傲。	Knowledge makes humble, ignorance makes proud.
活着,爲了學習。	Learn and live.
不學無術。	Learn not and know not.
過去的就讓它過去吧。	Let bygones be bygones.
別惹麻煩。	Let sleeping dogs lie.
泄漏天機。	Let the cat out of the bag.
謊言終究是謊言。	Lies can never changes fact.
人生如朝露。	Life is but a span.
書如其人。	Like author, like book.
有其父必有其子。	Like father, like son.
羊毛出在羊身上。	Like tree, like fruit.

一報還一報。	Like for like. Measure for measure.
三思而後行。	Look before you leap.
歲月既往，一去不回。	Lost time is never found again.
愛情是盲目的。	Love is blind.
没有妒忌就没有爱情。	Love is never without jealousy.
愛屋及烏。	Love me, love my dog.
勿失良機。	Make hay while the sun shines.
化敵爲友。	Make your enemy your friend.
謀事在人，成事在天。	Man proposes, God disposes.
禍不單行。	Misfortunes never come alone.
紙包不住火。	Murder will out.
需要是發明的動力。	Necessity is the mother of invention.
不要混水摸魚。	Never fish in trouble water.
永不言敗。	Never say die.
没有生而知之者。	No man is born wise or learned.
聰明一世，糊塗一時。	No man is wise at all times.
没有消息就是好消息。	No news is good news.
没有付出就没有收獲。	No pains, no gains.

没有不帶刺的玫瑰。	No rose without a thorn.
無火不生烟。	No smoke without fire.
勇者無懼。	No way is impossible to courage.
進攻是最好的防御。	Offense is the best defense.
一朝被蛇咬，十年怕井繩。	Once bitten, twice shy.
百聞不如一見。	One eyewitness is better than ten hearsays.
行善積德。	One good turn deserves another.
言爲心聲。	One´s words reflect one´s thinking.
苦盡甘來。	Pleasure comes through toil.
竹籃子打水一場空。	Pour water into a sieve.
熟能生巧。	Practice makes perfect.
預防勝于治療。	Prevention is better than cure.
驕傲使人落後。	Pride goes before, and shame comes after.
一諾千金。	Promise is debt.
要人尊敬,必須自重。	Respect yourself, or no one else will respect you.
羅馬偉業非一日之功。	Rome is not built in a day.
眼見爲實。	Seeing is believing.
說得容易,做得難。	Said is easier than done.

能言是銀，沉默是金。	Speech is silver, silence is gold.
静水常深。	Still water run deep.
堅持就是勝利。	Success belongs to the persevering.
既來之，則安之。	Take things as they come.
説曹操，曹操就到。	Talk of the devil and he will appear.
無私者無畏。	The best hearts are always the bravest.
偉人也有犯錯時。	The best man stumbles.
掩耳盜鈴。	The cat shuts its eyes when stealing.
燭臺底下最暗。	The darkest place is under the candlestick.
已成定局。	The die is cast.
早起的鳥兒有蟲吃。	The early bird catches the worm.
祇要目的正當，可以不擇手段。	The end justifies the means.
烈火驗真金，艱難磨意志。	The fire is the test of gold, adversity of strong man.
爬得高，摔得慘。	The higher up, the greater the fall.
本性難移。	The leopard cannot change its spots.
語言的巨人總是行動的矮子。	The greatest talkers are always least doers.
人越高尚，越謙虛。	The more noble, the more humble.
旁觀者清。	The outsider sees the most of the game.

五十步笑百步。	The pot calls the kettle black.
太陽也有黑點。	There are spots in the sun.
任何法規均有例外。	There is no general rule without some exception.
人言可畏。	The tongue is not steel, yet it cuts.
時不我待。	Time and tide wait for no man.
時間是醫治一切創傷的良藥。	Time cures all things.
光陰似箭。	Time flies.
時間就是金錢。	Time is money.
時光流逝，不可復得。	Time lost cannot be won again.
路遙知馬力，日久見人心。	Time tries all.
人非聖賢，孰能無過。	To err is human.
自由放任，一事無成。	Too much liberty spills all.
節約時間就是延長生命。	To save time is to lengthen life.
真理永存。	Truth never grows old.
團結就是力量。	Unity is strength.
吃小虧占大便宜。	Venture a small fish to catch a great one.
美德遠遠勝過美貌。	Virtue is fairer far than beauty.
滴水穿石。	Water dropping day by day wears the hardest rock away.

小心隔墻有耳。	Walls have ears.
好的開始,是成功的一半。	Well begun is half done.
井幹方知水可貴。	We never know the worth of water till the well is dry.
失者不可復得。	What´s lost is lost.
傷心舊事別重提。	When sorrow is asleep, wake it not.
欲求完美無缺的朋友必然成爲孤家寡人。	We shall never have friends if we expect to find them without fault.
自己的好事別去提,別人的恩惠要銘記。	We should never remember the benefits we have offered nor forget the favor received.
不管做什麼，都要一心一意。	Whatever you do, do with all your might.
酒後吐真言。	When wine is in truth, wit is out.
有志者事竟成。	Where there is a will, there is a way.
留得青山在，不怕没柴燒。	Where there is life, there is hope.
好人不長命。	Whom the gods love die young.
智者嘴在心裏，愚者心在嘴裏。	Wise man have their mouths in their hearts, fools have their hearts in their mouths.
勤工出巧匠。	Work makes the workman.
蠟燭不能兩頭點，精力不可過分耗。	You cannot burn the candle at both ends.

警告 / 提示
Warnings / Notices

注意！ Attention!

不可吃喝！ No eating and drinking!

請勿亂扔垃圾！ No littering!

小心狗！ Beware of Dog!

小心扒手！ Beware of pickpockets!

請保持小聲！ Keep your noise down!

停止！ Stop!

不可進入！ No entry!

小心頭！ Watch your head!

停車場 Parking Lot

緊急出口 Emergency Exit

不可停車！ No Parking!